GREECE

LONDON | NEW YORK
VISTA BOOKS | THE VIKING PRESS

Reprinted 1963
The original edition was published by Editions du Seuil, Paris.

GREECE

BY MIMICA CRANAKI

TRANSLATED BY NELINE C. CLEGG

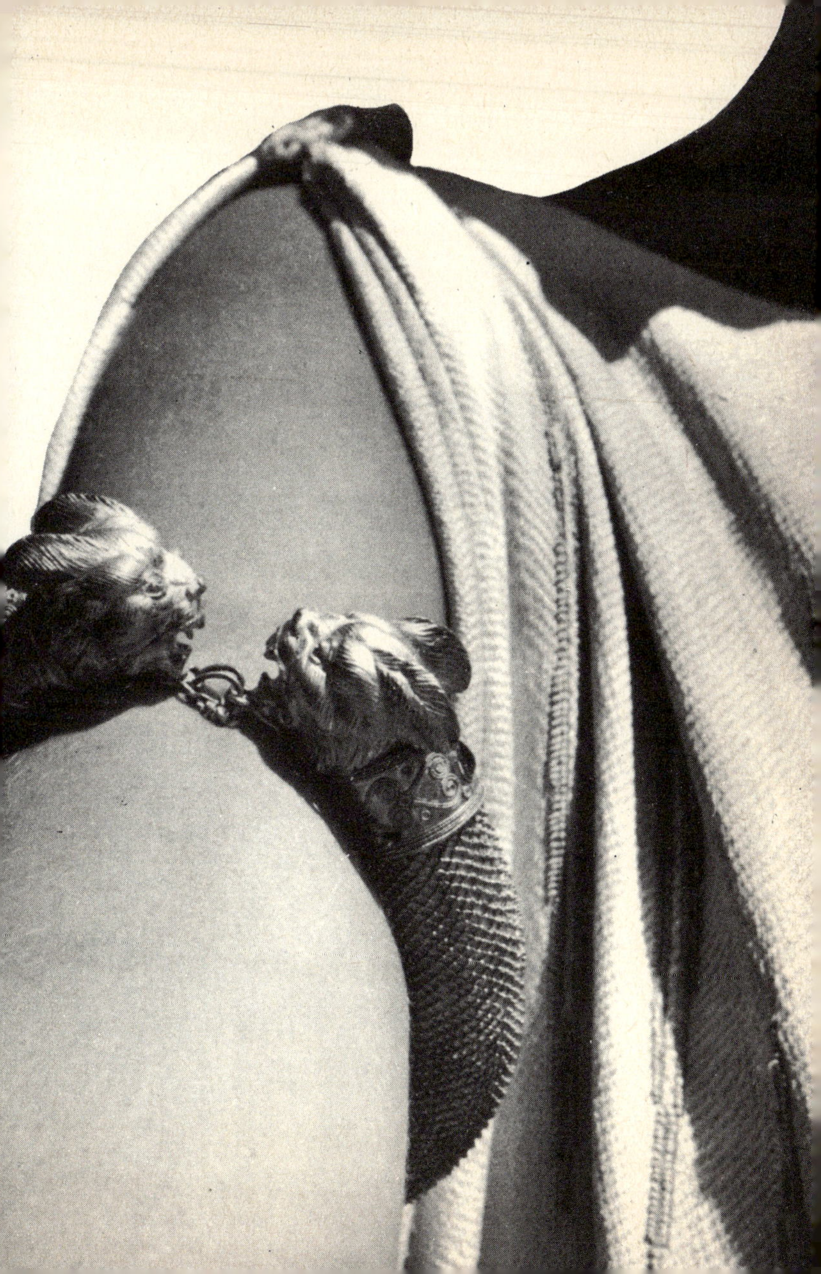

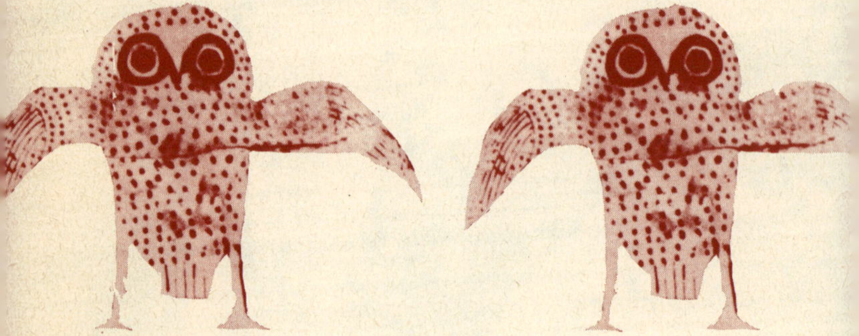

ARCHIMEDES

"Comes from this side of the world a great purple doom on the waters" [1]: from Pindar to Saint-John Perse the poets are in agreement. As everyone knows, in this part of the world men worked in marble, on philosophy and on their bodies. They knew almost as much as we do now, plus a secret which has probably been eroded away by the wear and tear of the centuries. Long ago, on this corner of the world Archimedes, that illustrious forerunner of the humanists, balanced his lever to lift the earth. He succeeded. Whether one calls it logos or miracle or anything you like, the delicate equilibrium of his lever has served as a standard for all human enterprise ever since.

The charm of Archimedes would seem to be very powerful, for it has managed to withstand the fascination of the Aztecs, the Incas and so many other pasts which have since come to light. Let's be just. The attraction of Greece is no doubt partly owing to its being so much closer to the centre of Western civilisation than Mexico both in space and time. But perhaps this has something to do with it, too: no matter how hard one pulls faces in front of the mirror, one can't get inside the skin of those exotic gods. With their four heads and five arms

[1] Saint-John Perse, *Anabasis,* translated by T. S. Eliot. London, Faber & Faber, 1930. New York, Harcourt, Brace & Co., 1938.

(or is it three?) they are like fortresses. On the other hand every one of us feels himself a little Promethean soul or a miniature Oedipus.

The first reaction, of course, is surprise. The country is just as you have always imagined it, with, in addition, the dust of the ages, which at times troubles the transparency of the air.

But no sooner have you thrown off the embrace of the violet hues, of the past, no sooner are you confronted with the present than you run up against some harsh truths, some problems which contradict your beautiful belief in humanity. For after all, where is Greece to be found? You have hoisted your sails, glorious as an Argonaut, and there you are, face to face with yourself once more. You meet machines which are neither the Trojan horse nor the statues of Daedalus, ordinary labourers bearing the names Themistocles or Pericles – a police apparatus which has nothing in common with the Erinnyes. You hear raucous surges of popular song escaping from the taverns and breaking upon the blackness of the streets; you are stifled by the misery, the suffering, the confusion. In short, you are immersed once more in history; and that is exactly what you have been trying to escape.

Where is Greece? As with Spanish inns, so with travels and countries: each person finds what he has brought. For the dyed-in-the-wool classicist the past encompasses all the present; thus the question does not arise. Greece, why, that's easy. The landscape plus a few old stones.

Now Greek nature lends itself even less than any other to such simplification. What connection is there between Attica and those desolate hills of the Occupation, like convicts, striped yellow and green by German camouflage? Yet the landscape was the same. And what are those Greek bays without their *lamparos?* [1] And what its moun-

[1] *lamparos:* fishing boats that go out at night with lamps to attract the fish.

tain paths without the little chapels where day and night little oil lamps burn in front of the icon of Saint Elias, the king of the peaks? Briefly, how can one separate the scenery from the people who live in it? Adoration of nature as such, devoid of human beings, is oriental or romantic – Greek it is certainly not. Socrates knew this when, in the Phaedrus, he added to his raptures about the Attic scenery: *"The men who dwell in the city are my teachers, and not the trees or the country."* [1]

By itself, nature is not sufficient to change a young man of today, even if he is a hero, into an Achilles. Rather the opposite occurs: human beings change their natural surroundings. But on this subject misconceptions are rife. Full of delight, a friend told me how, in the course of some hotel incident, she and her husband had been swindled by an "adorable little Greek shepherd" whose eyes "sparkled with Attic mischief." Out of a present-day little crook she had made an infant Odysseus.

Extremes meet, even in this land of the golden mean. This classicism, taken to the extreme, comes down to the same thing as the romanticism of the school of Leighton and Alma Tadema, of the lovers of the picturesque. Nowadays this is by far the most widespread variety. Greece died with its gods, declares one of those youngsters who has learnt nothing from his travels: *"Naively I was looking forward to fustanellas, ephebes, Turkish relics, Byzantine or oriental architecture – to tell the truth: the picturesque. And what do I see before me? A town just about as picturesque as Crewe . . . and everything else to match."*

True, as anywhere else, there is also a certain picturesqueness in

[1] Plato, *Phaedrus* par. 230. *The Dialogues of Plato,* translated by B. Jowett, Oxford University Press and Random House Inc., New York.

Greece; but it is not decorative, it has no artificial flower quality; it is permeated with tragedy, which makes it rather more difficult of access to the hasty tourist.

Anyway, what is the use of arbitrarily labelling something picturesque? What sense is there in this Procrustean effort to put yet another country on the bed of habit and ease, in order to strip it of all its riches and authenticity? I often ask myself this question, for my experience of my own country seldom tallies with the accounts of outside witnesses. What causes this incongruity?

To put it bluntly: it is the effect of an optical difference, of the fatal distortion active in the traveller's eye. Whatever view he takes of Greece, the tourist – be he a scholar or not – sees and judges at third hand. Which explains why his conclusions rarely coincide with the view obtained from first-hand experience. What to the inhabitant is a sacred gesture or a harrowing tragedy, in the eye of the foreign observer becomes a picturesque detail or a problem of economic fluctuation on a world scale. In the last resort this might be tantamount to allowing the most interested party no say in the matter at all. An impossible undertaking on this particular soil; dialogue is a Greek invention.

The second post-war era has brought another form of distortion: the righteous indignation of the professional protester, that beautiful spirit of the 20th century. Cliché is his strong point: thus, Greece is a fascist country. The resinated wine, the red mullets, the melons, they are all soaked in this totalitarian essence. All creatures on two legs are scoundrels who have sold themselves to the Americans. Of that there can be no doubt: otherwise they would be dead. Embedded in his monolithic dogmas, there's just one little detail our neo-Cato (I can see no Greek figure of this kind) overlooks: against whom is this fascism directed? It must have a counterpart, or it would have no meaning. Two are needed to make anything, even a totalitarian regime. That, too, is an invention of our august ancestors, and is called dialectics. Apparently it is not so easy to brutalize a people which has managed to emerge almost unscathed from four centuries of slavery . . .

But that is not all. There are still the petty bourgeois, the pervert, the German, the Teddy-boy, the sybarite, the photographer, the intellectual, the yachtsman and the like, each with his exclamations, his enthusiasms, his projections, his shams, his testimonies, his criticisms . . .

To them all Themistocles addressed his ancient saying: "Strike, but hear me."

CLIO

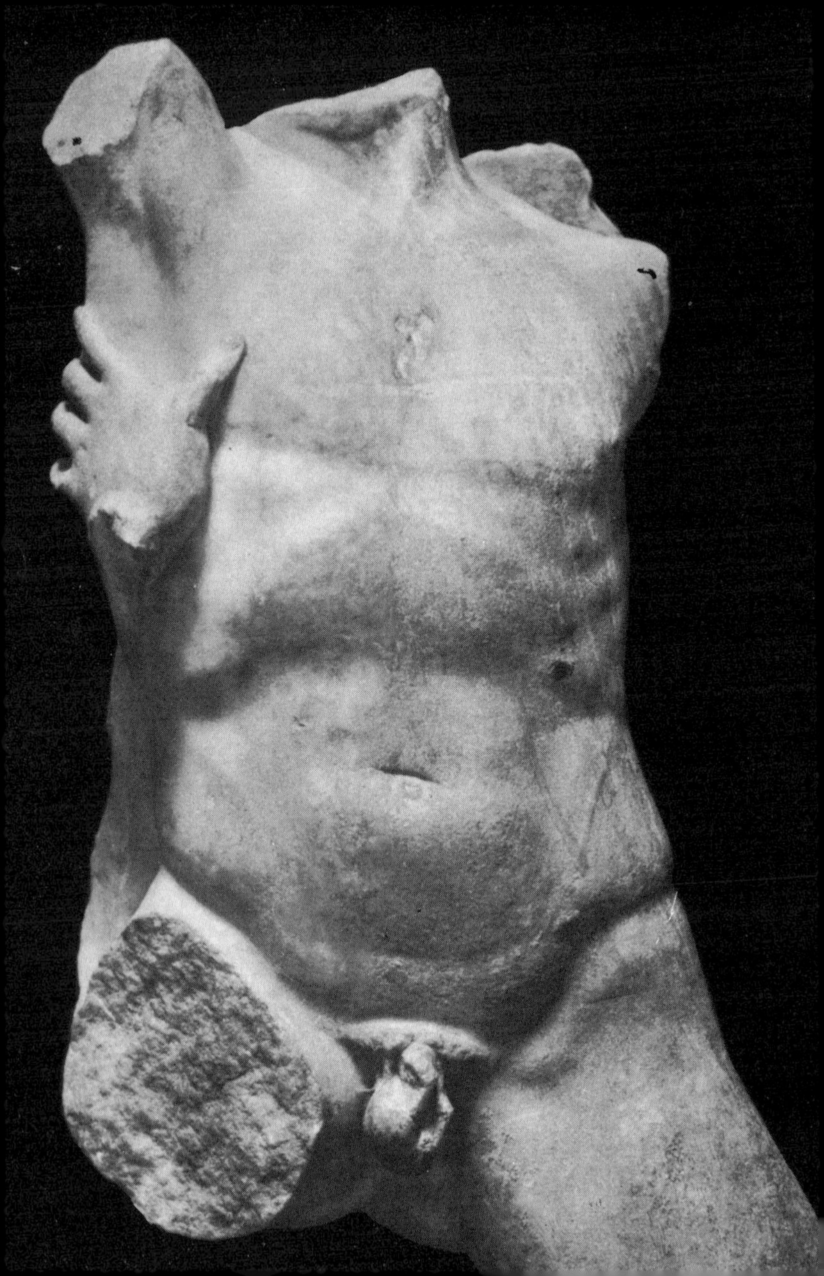

Pocket theogony

Undoubtedly the most precious invention of the Greeks, and one which distinguishes them profoundly from the Romans, is the myth. It implies infinitely more poetry, imagination and wisdom than a philosophic system, and that makes it more viable too.

Compare for example the *cosmogonies* (theories of the creation of the universe) of the pre-Socratic philosophers of the 7th century B.C., who of late have become fashionable again, to that of Hesiod (8th century B.C.). The philosophers hold up the universe to auction. What is the basic element of the world? Water, replies Thales. No, the infinite, suggests Anaximander. The infinite plus air, corrects Anaximenes. You don't understand a thing, declares Pythagoras, the mystic: it's number. It's the One, the pure Being, murmurs a choir of basses, those of the Eleates (Xenophanes, Parmenides, Zeno). Who can better that? The materialists of.course, Democritus and Leucippus, who make a higher bid with the atoms. Anaxagoras is going to put everybody in his place: *Nous,* reason, is the basic principle of the world. Bing! that sounds like the gong or like a knock-out blow.

Hesiod, after Homer the greatest poet of the most ancient period of Greece, takes a different line in his *Theogony* (the genealogy of the gods). Who made the world? The gods, obviously. And who made the gods? Love. Eros married Gaia (the Earth) to Uranus (Heaven) and from this union sprang a motley dozen of Titans and Titanesses. Moreover this conscientious couple brought to light three Cyclopes and the Hundred-handed Monsters.

"Brought to light" is a manner of speaking; for, in effect, Uranus denied his children all access to the light and kept them buried in the

depth of the earth. Gaia wanted to free them from paternal oppression and appealed to Cronos, the youngest of the Titans, for help (Cronos the crafty, says Hesiod). When night had fallen, Uranus, amorous as usual, was getting ready to go to bed with his wife when Cronos, with the slash of a sickle, cut off his testicles and threw them far away. The blood from the wound fell down on the earth, and fertilised it anew. Quite appropriately, this crime brought forth new monsters: the Erinnyes, the Giants and the Meliae Nymphs.

Like father, like son. Gaia had foretold that Cronos in his turn would be dethroned by one of his children. So by way of precaution he fell into the habit of devouring them as soon as they were born (Cronos = time). In this way he swallowed down half a dozen Olympians: Demeter, Hera, Poseidon, etc. When it was the turn of Zeus, his mother Rhea wanted to save the child. So she swaddled a stone which she gave her titanic husband to eat, and went to Mount Ida, on Crete, where she was delivered. The child grew up amongst the Curetes who danced the noisy Pyrrhic dance to drown its cries, and it drank the milk of the goat Amalthea. When his fostermother died, Zeus made a cuirass of her skin, the famous *Aegis*.

Zeus, this rebellious son of a terrible father, decided in his turn to dethrone Cronos. By a ruse he got him to take a drug, as a result of which he vomited up his children. That was the beginning of a Titanic struggle lasting ten years and ending in the victory of the Olympians (Zeus, Hera, Aphrodite, etc.). They remained in power for long centuries of prosperity, till the advent of Christianity; filling the chronicles with their scandals, adulteries, incests or bestialities.

After the gods, it was the turn of humans to be born.

According to the legend, there was once . . . a virtuous couple, Deucalion and Pyrrha. They lived in a society which, for all its antiquity, was all the more corrupt. So Zeus, like a good cryptopuritan, decided to drown them all in a great flood. However he advised the virtuous Deucalion to embark on an ark and to wait for his lightning and rain to subside. When the rains had ceased, Deucalion came out of his shelter and found himself alone with Pyrrha – quite alone, that is. So he implored Zeus to send him some companions. By way of reply the latter told him to throw "the bones of his mother" over his left shoulder. In those days men still had a feeling for words; Deucalion understood that in the highflown language of the gods "the bones of his mother" meant stones. He did as he was told; so did Pyrrha; and it is thus that human beings of both sexes came into the world.

In a less original way, Deucalion and Pyrrha had also begotten a son called Hellen; he again, without throwing stones, fathered three other sons – Doros, Xouthos and Aeolos. Xouthos begot Achaeus and Ion. Thus the picture was complete, all Greek tribes were accounted for. Doros – you've already guessed – became the ancestor of the Dorians. (They settled first in the centre of Greece, near Delphi, then crossed over to the Peloponnesus. This is the tribe of the Spartans.) The Aeolians settled in Thessaly. Achaeus produced the Achaeans. The Ionians first occupied Attica; thence they moved to the shore of Asia Minor, to that region which would later be called Ionia. They played a major part in the history of Greece.

The age of reason

All legend is legend about something; in other words it is the poetical version of a piece of prose, of a more or less documented historical fact. On the level of history all the ado about Deucalion's offspring coincided roughly with the settlement of the Dorians in the Peloponnesus (1100 B.C.). Their reception cannot have been particularly friendly. For the thick walls of Tiryns, which because of their size were called "cyclopean" and whose ruins still impress us today, show that the Dorians met with considerable resistance from the Mycenaeans. This was a reversal of roles and a just retribution, for about 1400 B.C. Mycenaean civilisation itself had taken the place of that of Crete by means of fire and blood. Today in the Palace of Phaestos, which was once quite white, one can still see the traces of the fire which consumed it.

Before the coming of the Dorians the Mycenaeans must have had great prestige, for the famous crusade which united all the Achaeans against the town of Troy took place under the command of a Mycenaean chieftain, Agamemnon. Through the sonorous hexameters of the *Iliad* and the *Odyssey* this pageant of demi-gods, made immortal by the poetic genius of Homer, marches by. At the head are Agamemnon and Menelaus, the two Atrides, tribal kings. And then comes Achilles, the beautiful, quick-footed youth, ennobled by an early death and followed by the shadow of his friend Patrocles. Next are the "divine" Odysseus, the figurehead of Adventure, and Ajax the strong. On the other side of the barricade is the royal family: the old couple Priam and Hecuba, and the younger pair Hector and Andromache, plus the youngster Polyxenes. They hear, knocking at the door, the

◀ Apollo

The transformations of Odysseus.

Three stages in the immortality of Odysseus the Wily and Circe the Vamp:
The Vase,
The Comic Strip,
and the Film.

fate which will later be revealed in classic tragedy.

In the Odyssey, on the other hand, the characters are less dramatic and more edifying. The vamp Circe reduces all men to the status of swine. Calypso embodies the seductive appeal of the extramarital adventure which, sooner or later, is bound to end in disaster. As to the Cyclops Polyphemus, personifying brutal force – Odysseus succeeds in getting the better of him by sheer guile. His reward awaits him in Ithaca: in the arms of the faithful Penelope who has managed to keep her suitors at a distance by applying herself day and night to her weaving, always making and unmaking the same cloth. The happy ending is complete.

It is impossible to fix the time of the Trojan war. Early 14th, middle or end of the 13th century B.C.? The date remains uncertain. Yet there seems to be little question that the epics of the *Iliad* and the *Odyssey* had a long existence as ballads before being assembled by Homer; various additions were inserted up to the time of the edition compiled in Athens, in the second half of the 6th century. It is also held that the poems took shape largely in the 8th century, with an interval of about fifty years between the older *Iliad* and the more recent *Odyssey*.

In any case there can be no doubt that at the beginning of the 8th century the "dark age of Greece" had come to an end and a glimmer of light had appeared. It was the dawn of classical Greece.

What, by the crudest compression of history, is called "Greek civilisation" is centred in the two cities of Athens and Sparta.

Athens was the example of the Ionian city-state, the *polis* par excellence. In Sparta, where in the words of Pindar law reigned supreme over all, immortals as well as mortals, the Dorian spirit was incarnated. One particular legend out of thousands will clearly illustrate the warlike temper of the Spartans which has since become proverbial. Cadmus, who was of Phoenician origin and, if Herodotus is to be believed, invented the alphabet, was also the founder of Thebes (every Greek city-state had its heroic founder). To clear the site he had to kill a dragon on the very spot where the town was to rise. Thereupon Athena appeared and counselled him to sow the dragon's teeth in the earth. From them armed warriors sprang up, who immediately set about killing each other. Only five survived, and these were the founders of the tribe of the *Sparti* (= the sown men).

Thus the famous "laconism", nowadays a synonym for conciseness and brevity, is derived from the fact that those rustic Lacedemonians (*lakon* was another Greek word for Spartan) did not have very delicate feelings to express, nor too complicated ideas.

The historical period of Sparta began with the legislation of Lycurgus, a character on the border between history and legend. He divided the land of Laconia by lots among the inhabitants, whom he grouped into three classes: first the *perioikoi* (provincials), second, the *ilotes* (slaves) and third, the Spartans. The system, founded on asceticism and an iron discipline, which has been wrongly likened to the German mentality, quickly bore fruit. Sparta began by swallowing the adjoining province of Messina. Then it extended its supremacy over the whole of the Peloponnesus. In short, in the 5th century, the clash with Athens, which had expanded its power on the other side of the Corinthian isthmus, became unavoidable.

The sudden flowering of 5th-century Athens came about in a different way. Like Rome, Athens at first was subject to the rule of a king; but kings were abolished about 1045 B.C. Like Rome, Athens had it's founder hero: Theseus. It also had its Lycurgus in the person of the severe Dracon (7th century) who, it is said, imposed one single penalty for all crimes: death. But it was Solon who laid the foundations of what in the 5th century was the Athenian republic. He divided the citizens into four classes – in the strict sense of the word – according to the role they played in the productive process, i.e. according to their wealth. This sage also instituted the Areopagus (Tribunal), and the Senate *(Bouli)* which drafted the laws and sent them as proposals to the Assembly of the People.

Yet in spite of Solon's wisdom it took Athens a long time to achieve the democracy for which it became famed. It had to pass through the whole gamut of constitutions and abortive experiments enumerated by Aristotle in his *Politics:* first heroic kingship, which ended with Kodros; next aristocracy and oligarchy with the Alcmaeonidae, a noble and perpetually trouble-making family; and finally tyranny, under Peisistratus and subsequently under his sons Hipparchus and Hippias. The "tyrannicides" Harmodius and Aristogeiton freed the city from the Tyrants. You can see these young and ardent upholders of justice in the museum at Naples: with sword uplifted, about to deal a blow. Cleisthenes benefited from this political murder. He reformed Solon's constitution and made the Assembly pass the law on ostracism (exile), so called because the vote was exercised by means of a shell *(ostrakon)*. The Athenians made an impressive use of it. Not one statesman escaped ostracism; not even Aristides the Just.

All heroes have to show their mettle, accomplishing fabulous deeds before winning the hand of a fair lady. Athens had to defeat the Persians before it could win its Golden Age.

The prelude to the wars with Persia was the rebellion of the Ionian colonies in Asia Minor. You will remember how the Ionians, after they had left Attica on the Greek mainland, founded a chain of flourishing Greek cities on the coast of Asia Minor. Between the 10th and the 5th century B.C. these colonies prospered and for that very reason became a source of worry and vexation to the Great King of

GREEK LITTLE

HERAKLES

ACHILLES

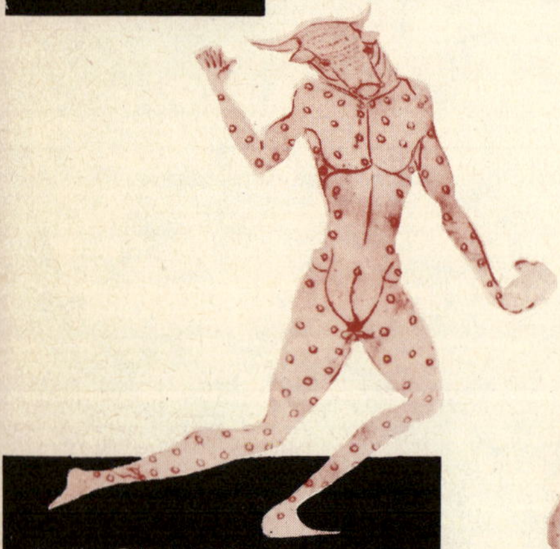

MINOTAUR

CENTAUR

HEATRE 1 Ancient Characters

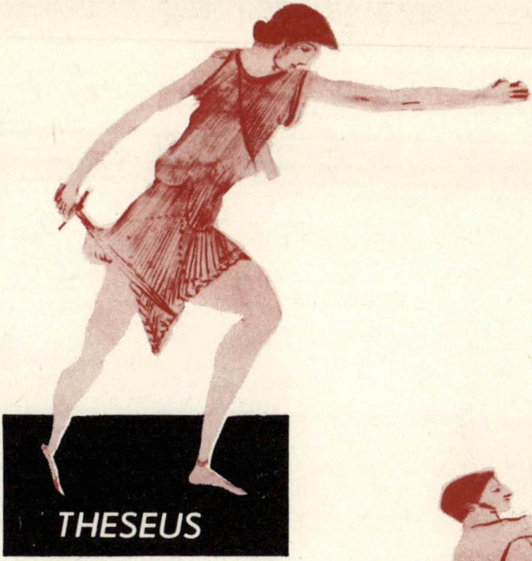

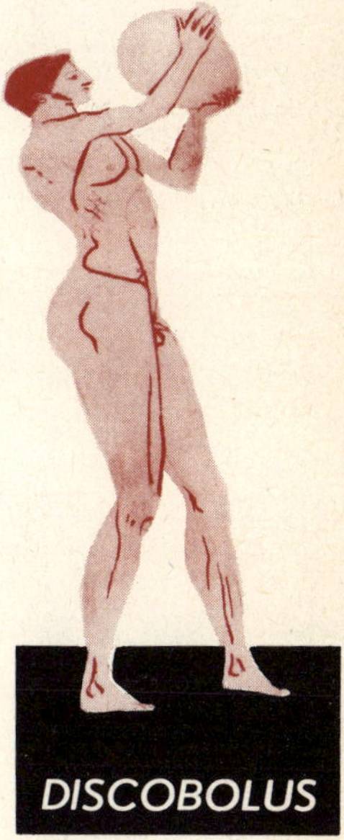

Persia, who then controlled Asia Minor. Wishing to protect his *Lebensraum*, and once and for all to have done with both Athens and its colonies, Darius began by conquering the latter. Next, he sent an army of 100,000 foot-soldiers and 10,000 horsemen under the command of Datis and Artaphernes to Greece. The encounter which ensued at Marathon (490 B.C.) was the struggle between Polyphemus and Odysseus all over again. Under the plan drawn up by Miltiades, the Athenians, assisted by the Plataeans, had concentrated their forces on both extreme flanks. When the Persians attacked, the Athenians and their allies split into two groups which made quick work of encircling the enemy and putting him to flight, pursuing him to the sea. "*Cynegirus, too, the son of Euphorion,*" relates Herodotus, the historian of the Median (Persian) wars, "*had his hand cut off with an axe as he was getting hold of a ship's stern, and so lost his life.*" [1] This hero was the brother of Aeschylus, who also fought at Marathon.

Part of the booty of Marathon was used to erect the statue of Athena Promachos; another to swell the treasury of Delphi. The first act of the Persian wars was over.

Ten years later Xerxes led another important army into Greece. This time the destiny of all Hellas was put in jeopardy at the pass of Thermopylae. Betrayed by Ephialtes who showed the Persians a way through the mountains, 300 Spartans, Thebans and Thespians under the command of Leonidas perished to the last man.

While the Spartans were dying at Thermopylae in obedience to their laws, Themistocles conducted a dramatic struggle in Athens. "The wooden wall will save the town", the Pythia (prophetic priestess at Delphi) had predicted in her usual Sibylline manner, and the majority of Athenians believed that this referred to the walls of the Acropolis. But Themistocles interpreted the oracle differently: the wooden wall, why, that clearly was a symbol for the fleet which accounted for Athens' strength. He had great difficulty in convincing his fellow-citizens but finally won the day, and the Athenian fleet met that of Xerxes in the Straits of Salamis. Aeschylus has given us a famous account of this battle in his *Persians*, through the mouth of the Messenger who brings news from Greece to Queen Atossa in Persia:

"*But when fair day with milk-white steeds appeared*
And covered all the land with gladdening rays,
Then rose from that Greek armament a song
Both loud and musical, and the island rocks
Re-echoed, shouting battle. On our side

[1] Herodotus, *The Histories*, Translated by Aubrey de Selincourt. Book Six p. 402 (113). Penguin Classics.

The age of reason

Fell disappointment, wonder and dismay,
Shattering the general hope. Not as for flight
Pealed forth the Hellenes that high Paean-hymn,
But with good courage rallying to the fray.
All yonder side blazed with the trumpet's blare.
Then with one impulse, at the pilot's word,
All oars were dipped and smote the seething brine,
And swiftly their whole battle hove in view.
Their right wing in good order led the way,
Then all their navy followed; then one heard
A cry that grew: "Sons of Hellenes, on!
Save Hellas, save your children, save your wives,
Your fathers' graves, the temples of their gods,
From slavery! Fight, to defend your all!"
Then from a sea of Persian voices roared
The counter clamour. For the hour was come.
Now ship smote ship with brazen-pointed prow.
A Greek began that onslaught, tearing off
All the ornature from a Sidonian hull.
Then on and on, with ships for spears, they fought.
The Persian fleet, in a perpetual stream,
At first appeared invincible; but when
Their numbers in the narrows packed and hemmed
Grew dense, they cracked their oarage in the crowd,
And smote each other with their beaks of brass,
And none might help his fellow. 'Ware of this,
The Grecian shipmasters with cunning skill
Jostled us round and round, – till hulls capsized,
And all the sea was hidden from our sight,

With wrecks and human carnage covered o'er.
The cliffs and jutting reefs were thronged with dead,
And every vessel left in the Asian fleet
Rowed hard for safety in disordered rout." [1]

From these wars Athens emerged as a great naval power. Themistocles fortified the city with long ramparts, and a maritime league was formed under Athenian hegemony. Beneath the captured trophies of the opulent Medes the great Age of Athens flourished. It resounded with the steps of Sophocles, Aeschylus, Euripides, Phidias, Herodotus, Thucydides, Hippocrates, Aristophanes, Socrates, Plato, Xenophon. This polished century, smooth as marble, brought to perfection two of the most infernal contrivances of mankind: tragedy and philosophy. Henceforth all human history bears the imprint of one of these two aspects. Now it takes on its dramatic character, that of the hero of the stage; then that of the thinker who tries to reflect, to discover a meaning in what his double has just accomplished. The characters in Sophocles, Aeschylus and Euripides are developed and completed in the works of Plato and even in the more abstract works of Aristotle. Take for example the tragedy of Prometheus. It recurs on a different plane as the central problem of Plato's philosophy: whether a connection is possible between Reality and the world of appearances; and if so, how. The ultimate answer to this question is quite surprising: the link is Promethean fire, that spark which spurts up "suddenly", no one knows how or why, and which does not properly belong to the province of philosophy. This is how Plato puts it in his extraordinary "Seventh Letter", where the essence of his political thought is to be found. Another example is that of Antigone, of the conflict between the individual and the State. On the level of tragedy this conflict is insoluble. But for the philosopher, tragedy becomes problem. Plato, who through his mother was related to Solon and through his father to Kodros, the last king of Athens – Plato whom everything seemed to have destined for politics, put this problem into the centre of his philosophy. In his *Republic* he offers his famous solution. The contradiction between the individual, between the thirst for the absolute which consumes Antigone, and the world of compromise which makes up the State, cannot be resolved "*until,*" adds Plato, "*philosophers are kings, or the kings and princes of this world have the spirit and power of philosophy, and political greatness and wisdom meet in one.*" [2]

That means that the Greek *polis* (City-State), that work of art, as

[1] Aeschylus, *The Persians,* Seven Plays in English Verse, by Lewis Campbell, M.A. The World's Classics, Oxford University Press, 1938.
[2] Plato, *The Republic,* V, par. 473, (p. 737 Random House ed.).

Hegel called it, was no longer able to satisfy Plato, who witnessed its greatness and its decline. He was, in fact, born in the year that Pericles died: 429 B.C.

Criticism of the city-state and the crisis to which this gave rise was the work of the Sophists (Protagoras, Prodikos, etc.). They destroyed the prestige of law and of objectivity in general by means of an adroit and eloquent scepticism, culminating in the famous formula: "Man is the measure of all things." The grave danger of such teachings for the city-state was shown by the death-sentence passed on Socrates – an act which has tarnished Athenian fame forever. What was the accusation brought against him? The introduction of new gods, in particular of that scandalous deity whose heir was to be Christianity: the individual. Socrates drank poison not as a hero, but as a philosopher. His death, in 399 B.C., has been described in the *Phaedo*, a testament to the immortality of the human soul which has never since been equalled.

Pericles, the son of Xanthippe, strove to organise the supremacy of Athens and to add to his own glory. Helped by such artists as Phidias, Ictinos and Callicrates he had the main buildings of the Acropolis constructed, thus turning his century into a golden age in every sense. Artistically, this was the outcome of a long period of preparation going back beyond Hellenic times proper, to the civilisations of Crete and Mycenae. The Greek temple is the direct heir of the Mycenaean *megaron* (palace). It assumed its definite shape, with sloping roofs and pediment, round about the 8th century. The older Doric temple rested on thick, straight columns. The Ionian style went in for more slender columns and curved-in capitals. The later Corinthian manner gave the capital an acanthus shape.

These temples in turn gave birth to sculpture, as of course they had to shelter the gods. Statues of men began to replace the earlier wooden idols *(xoana)* once Daedalus, according to legend, had released their arms and legs – that is to say, had conferred a human form on them. The smile of the earliest archaic statues expresses the amused surprise of a human being who, after the long sleep of eternity, awakes to the world. Malraux took pleasure in pointing him out each time he encountered him in the history of art: "*Far more than in its smoothly flowing drapery, all Hellas is in the curves of these faintly pouting lips (which somehow bring to mind the Odyssey) – curves that were to last until Praxiteles, who used them to suggest the mystery of man. Of man, not of the cosmos; for this smile is different from that of the Angkor figures. Whenever it recurs, something of Greece is on the point of breaking into flower – whether in the smiling grace of Rheims or that of the Virgin of the Rocks; whenever man comes into his kingdom he regains his precarious sway over that domain, limited but rich*

"the amused smile of a human being who awakes to the world..." ▶

Attic cup

in imitations, which he conquered for the first time on the Acropolis of Delphi."

The star of Athens began to wane about 431 B.C., the date on which the Peloponnesian war – that other thirty-years war – broke out. "*The real cause I consider to be*" declares Thucydides after having lengthily explained its preliminaries, "*the one which was formerly most kept out of sight. The growth of the power of Athens, and the alarm which this inspired in Lacedemon, made war inevitable.*"[1] The famous Epitaph of Pericles, which is reported by Thucydides (the historian of the Peloponnesian war), was pronounced in honour of the first victims of this war. It is both a funeral oration and a hymn of praise to the city-state for which those heroes had fought.

It was also Pericles' own epitaph. Shortly afterwards he died of the

[1] Thucydides, *The History of the Peloponnesian War,* Translated by Richard Crawley. Everyman's Library. London J. M. Dent & Sons Ltd., New York, E. P. Dutton & Co. Inc. Vol. I, p. 81.

plague which wrought such ravages in Athens (429). An armistice, signed in 421, granted the belligerents a few years' respite. These years are filled with the words and deeds of the handsome Alcibiades and with the disastrous expedition to Sicily which he commanded and which he betrayed by fleeing to the Peloponnesus. The naval battle of Aegos Potamos (405) put an end both to the war and to the naval supremacy of Athens. Lysander, the Spartan admiral, entered the harbour of Piraeus in triumph.

Yet the formidable military might of Sparta was defeated by a new star, brilliant though ephemeral: the town of Thebes. With the final decline of the Greek world Boeotia thus had its moment of glamour. Thebes gave to Greece not only Pindar, but two first-rate generals as well – Epaminondas and Pelopidas.

The hour of Macedonia had struck. The Hellenes were united for the last time by Philip and his son Alexander in a noble effort to Hellenise the Asian barbarians. Union, so they say, is strength. Some obstacles had however to be overcome: first Philip of Macedonia had to crush the resistance of the Athenians and the eloquence of Demosthenes. At Chaeronaea the Macedonian army inflicted a bloody defeat on the Hellenes (338). "*Their tomb has no inscription,*" said Pausanias, "*but is surmounted by a lion, probably a reference to the spirit of the men. That there is no inscription is, in my opinion, because their courage was not favoured by appropriate good fortune.*"[1] Today the lion of Chaeronaea, that symbol of vain courage, is coated with the dust of the Athens-Làrissa road. Storks nest on its head, transforming the savage beast into a domestic pet.

The reign of Alexander the Great lasted scarcely thirteen years. And so the dawn and the twilight of Hellenic times are symmetrically incarnated in two youths: Achilles and Alexander. The latter was probably well aware of the role history and aesthetics had assigned to him: before setting out on his campaign against the Persians he made a pilgrimage to the tomb of Achilles whom, according to Arrian, he envied "*for having had Homer to sing his fame.*"

But Alexander was no less to be envied; for he had as tutor Aristotle, the most powerful mind of Greece. The extent of the latter's power can be measured by the fact, among others, that the assimilation of his thought by theology during long centuries of medieval scholasticism, nevertheless left intact the permanent foundations of his ancient wisdom. His *Metaphysics*, his *Politics* and his *Nicomachean Ethics* are documents of the greatest topicality.

[1] Pausanias, *Description of Greece*. Translated by W. H. S. Jones, M.A. London, William Heinemann Ltd., New York, G. P. Putnam & Sons, 1918. Vol. IV p. 361 (IX, x1 par. 10).

The age of reason

Alexander's march to Asia was marked by a series of brilliant victories: the victory of the river Granicus, and those of Issus (333) and Gaugamela opened the way to India. However, at the gates of India the army lost its wind, and Alexander was forced to turn back. He was never to see Macedonia again and died in 323, at the age of 33, in Babylon.

The news of his death provoked all sorts of disorder: the Hellenes, who had followed the Macedonians only reluctantly, took new courage and grew restive. Aristotle, who happened to be in Athens, fled to Chalcis – in order to save the Athenians (as he put it, referring to Socrates' death) from committing yet another crime against philosophy.

The wars of the Diadochs (= successors), which brought in their wake the dismemberment of the Macedonian empire, inaugurated the period of Hellenism – the first "ism", the first imitation in history. The name is derived from *Hellenists,* those Middle-Eastern people who adopted Greek ways, in particular to Hellenised Jews. Seleucos founded the kingdom of the Seleucids in Asia; Ptolemy that of the Ptolemies in Egypt. Hellenism flourished in the shadow of the former ages of greatness.

So – in the words of the modern poet Cavafy – the only thing to do in the circumstances was to await the arrival of the barbarians. And they did not keep history waiting long. In 146 Greece became a Roman province. Pompey put an end to the Greek state of Syria and Octavius, at Actium, to that of Ptolemaic Egypt.

The Roman poet Horace described the new situation kindly: conquered Greece vanquished the conqueror by other, more indirect means. Be this as it may, from this moment the Prosaic and the Earnest, in other words Law and Order, solemnly enter into history. Creon gets the better of Antigone.

Certain periods of history resemble holiday beaches: they flourish only in summer sunshine. So it was with Greece, province of Rome.

But summer returns, something is stirring in the stagnant waters. Who is that tall silhouette on the hill of the Areopagus whose passionate gestures are trying to shake the Assembly of decadent pagans out of its torpor? Of what religion is this stranger the apostle? "Ye men of Athens," said St. Paul, "I perceive that in all things ye are too superstitious. For as I passed by, and beheld your devotions, I found an altar with this inscription, TO THE UNKNOWN GOD. Whom therefore ye ignorantly worship, him declare I unto ye." This time Socrates no longer stood alone against the city-state. Upheld by the faith of the early Christians, the Apostle of the Gentiles denounced the false gods of Idolatry with a new force: "Forasmuch then as we are the offspring of God, we ought not to think that the Godhead is like unto gold, or silver, or stone, graven by art and man's device. And the times of this ignorance God winked at; but now commandeth all men everywhere to repent; because he hath appointed a day, in the which he will judge the world in righteousness by that man whom he hath ordained; whereof he hath given assurance to all men, in that he hath raised him from the dead."

"And when they heard of the resurrection of the dead, some mocked: and others said, 'We will hear thee again of this matter.' So Paul departed from among them. Howbeit certain men clave unto him, and believed: among the which was Dionysius the Areopagite, and a woman named Damaris, and others with them."

Dionysius the Aeropagite is still the patron saint of Athens, and his feast, the 3rd of October, one of the biggest celebrations of the year.

St. Paul was more successful in Corinth. In the First Epistle to the Corinthians Plato's voice has dwindled to a mere murmur. Like the rays of a sun which has already sunk below the horizon one can still, in the background, make out the parable of the cave from his *Republic*. "When I was a child, I spoke as a child, I understood as a child, I thought as a child: but when I became a man, I put away childish things. For now we see through a glass, darkly; but then face to face: now I know in part; but then I shall know even as also I am known."

Dionysius the Areopagite was one of the first Church Fathers, that is, one of the immediate successors of the Apostles. After them came the later Church Fathers who undertook the struggle against Jews, heretics and pagans. The Alexandrian school (Clement and Dionysius of Alexandria, Origen, etc.) attempted a fusion between neo-Platonism and Christian doctrine. But the great period of Christian literature did not start until A.D. 325 – the year of the first Council of Nicea which, in the contest with the Arian heresy, formulated the first articles of the Creed. From the Alexandrian school came Athanasius, the formidable and effective opponent of Arius; Basil the Great (the first saint of the year in the Orthodox calendar); Gregory of Nyssa and Gregory of Nazianza; St. John Chrysostom was of the school of Antioch. As St. John the Baptist was persecuted by King Herod, so this eloquent defender of Christianity was hounded by the Empress Eudoxia. His oratorical gifts and his popularity could not save him from exile, nor from that authoritarian woman's persecution. Byzantium had not yet given Orthodoxy the freedom of the city.

But let's proceed in an orderly fashion.

Byzantium

One has to be a Voltaire to make a virtue of necessity, and to turn prejudice and ignorance into wit. One must also have the fortune to belong to the 18th century. Since then, a lot of water has run under the bridges; history, including that of Byzantium, has left its marks. How can one hope to understand anything about 20th-century Greece except against the background of those seemingly endless middle ages which are still flowing into the present?

The connection, moreover, goes back much further than one might expect: Byzantium was a colony of Megara (and therefore Greek), founded by Byzes in the 7th century B.C. Thus the Greece-Byzantium-Greece chain turns full circle. Here in 330 A.D. Constantine, who owes his epithet the Great partly at least to this happy idea, inaugurated the new capital of the Roman empire, thereby changing it into a Christian empire. A few years earlier (in 313) the Edict of Milan had made a decisive step in that direction by proclaiming Christianity the official religion. The centre of gravity slowly moved from West to East and at the same time the capital found itself sheltered from the barbarian invasions, at any rate those from the North. For in the end that Eastern empire succumbed to the blows of two enemies: first, the attacks of the Eastern barbarians, the oriental hordes which after the 7th century ceaselessly hurled themselves at Byzantium. But the other, the more dangerous and pernicious enemy, was division in the Church, those religious struggles which took the dimensions of real civil wars.

The four seasons of the Byzantine empire were the Justinian spring (6th century), the summer of the Isaurian dynasty (717—867), the

◄ St. Demetrius. Byzantine painting, 17th century

reign of the Macedonian dynasty (867—1081), and the period of the Crusades (1081—1261) which preceded the final fall of the empire.

Between Constantine and Justinian a score of emperors followed each other. There's no need to memorise them all. Two, however, one will have to note: Theodosius I, whose death coincided with the final division of the Roman empire into two parts (the empire of the West hardly survived this split); and Julian the Apostate who, as his nickname indicates, tried to restore paganism. He reopened the temples and even consulted the oracle at Delphi. On that occasion the Pythia, so it is said, uttered her famous Swan Song: "*Go and tell the king that the beautiful palace has fallen to the ground. Phoebus no longer possesses so much as a hovel, no longer any prophetic laurels, no longer a melodious spring. The water that spoke has been killed.*"

As always, the Pythia's prophecy proved to be correct. The pagan interlude was without sequel. Julian perished quite young (in 363) on an expedition against the Persians. Thirty years later an edict of Theodosius II finally prohibited paganism and again closed the temples. The Olympic Games were suppressed (393), so were the mysteries at Eleusis.

Then came the Great Age of Byzantium, with its Roi-Soleil Justinian who ascended the throne in 527. Justinian married beneath him: the daughter of a bear-keeper of the Hippodrome called Theodora. You can admire them both, solemnly and ceremoniously facing each other, as they have been immortalised in that extraordinary mosaic of San Vitale, in Ravenna. How do they come to be there? They pursued a dream not without grandeur: to restore the Roman empire; and really, at that time the idea did not seem too utopian. They nearly brought it off. Generals like Belisarius and Narsis took part of the coast of Africa, Southern Italy and a part of Spain. But to conquer is one thing, to hold is another. A few years later nothing remained of these successes but a memory.

Justinian's vision was great in all respects: his legislative work, due to the genius of the jurist Tribonian, has survived all political and social changes in Europe; so that Roman law as codified by him has for centuries formed the structure of the modern world. What was later to be called the *corpus juris civilis* (corpus of civil law) consists of four parts, three of which (the Codex, the Pandects and the Institutions) were written in Latin and the fourth, the Novellae, in Greek.

But the main testimony to the greatness of this age and its emperor is the Church of St. Sophia, opened in 537 and built by two architects from Asia Minor: Anthemius and Isidorus. This was the masterpiece of Byzantine architecture (cruciform and surmounted by a dome). Even Justinian was dazzled by so much magnificence: "I have surpassed you, Solomon," he exclaimed when he entered the Church on the inaugural day.

With Heraclius (crowned in 610) the Byzantine era proper started: this strange empire was no longer a Roman, but a *Greek empire of the East*. The use of Greek in official documents proves this, as does the Hellenisation of the language (Heraclius took for himself the title of *Basileus*, i.e., King). Empire *of the East* – for the 7th century witnessed the downfall of the Roman empire of the West. One after the other, the conquests of Justinian passed into the hands of the barbarians. Heraclius had successively to repulse the attacks of Persians, Slavs, and finally Arabs who pressed forward throughout the 7th century. What was left of Byzantium? Little enough indeed compared with the ambitious dreams of Justinian: only Greece, and Asia Minor. Greece now was subjected to massive Slav penetration. From these Slav incursions Fallmerayer later drew the main arguments for his famous theory of the "slavisation" of the Greeks. We will return to this later. Thus the empire's territory was mainly restricted to Asia Minor. The East became a factor of the first importance and increasingly set the pace in politics and administration. It is very significant that the dynasties which followed that of Heraclius were without exception of oriental origin. This was true of the Isaurian dynasty, and again of the so-called "Macedonian" dynasty which, in fact, came from Armenia.

The reign of the Isaurian emperors was marked by a most extraordinary movement, that of the Iconoclasts (literally: effigy-smashers). What did it signify? Was it an anticipation of the Reformation, as one might not unreasonably argue? Was it a reaction against a new form of idolatry – that of the icons – which sometimes bordered on fetichism and which was so well suited to the passive souls of the Byzantines? Formal labels cannot do sufficient justice to this complex movement. In any case the Iconoclastic emperors were enlightened rationalists, and that, for Byzantium, was in itself enough to spell trouble.

The emperor Leo III, a Lutheran before Luther, published in 725 an edict prohibiting icons, the cult of which had degenerated into real idolatry. The empress Irene the Athenian restored them at the seventh and last Oecumenical Council of Nicea, in 787 – which did not restrain this bigot from tearing out her son's eyes three years later, so as to reign in his place. But after her death the Iconoclast feud flared up again. And it was again a woman, Theodora, who re-established the effigies, this time for good. On the 11th March, 843 – a date still commemorated by the Greek Church – a ceremony in St. Sophia celebrated the "rehabilitation of orthodoxy".

The period of the Macedonian emperors was above all military. The frontiers of the empire were extended, and Basil II, nicknamed the Bulgaroctone (Bulgarian-catcher), won a decisive victory over the Bulgarians who, from the 7th century onwards, had seriously threatened the empire. The Bulgarian army was destroyed and Basil took 15,000 prisoners. He had their eyes gouged out, with the exception of one man out of every hundred, who was allowed to keep one eye in order to take his comrades back to King Samuel. All these exploits, and others of a similar nature, provide the subject matter of a children's book, *the* book for Greek children, which bears the title *In the Days of Bulgaroctone* and brings tears to the eyes of all brats who read it. The Bulgarian still is enemy number one. After him comes the Turk. None of this makes the task of the Atlantic Community any easier.

The schism between the Orthodox Church and the Pope now grew wider. The story reminds one a little of Mark Twain's twins. The famous humourist tells how he had a twin brother. One day the nurse washed them both together in the bath-tub, and one was drowned. "I have never been able to make out whether it was my brother or me" adds Mark Twain. Which of the two is the schismatic, the Pope or the Patriarch? Who has excommunicated whom? A first mutual excommunication took place in the second half of the 9th century. The Patriarch (Photius) reproached the Pope for demanding celibacy of his priests. (Greek popes, i.e. priests, can marry and are generally fathers of large families); for allowing young children to drink milk and eat cheese; and – a much more serious offence – for adding the *Filioque* to the Creed, thus setting up a distinction between the nature of the Father and that of the Son. The schism became complete two centuries later, by a new excommunication, again reciprocal. This downright struggle for prestige had nonetheless a deeper cause: the rivalry between the Pope and the Patriarch in Southern Italy, where those two authorities clashed with each other, each trying to take more than his share and to increase his influence.

In due time the Crusaders arrived to hasten the disintegration of the empire. We will pass over the first three Crusades, whose failure has wrongly been blamed on the lethargy and duplicity of the Byzantine Emperor. Let's rather say a few words about the fourth, which met with an unquestioned succes. True, it didn't end in the capture of Jerusalem but, a minor detail, in that of Constantinople (in 1204). Equally true it was led by Boniface of Montferrat, by Pope Innocent III and by the Doge of Venice, Dandolo. And Venice in those days was an economic power which tended to reinforce its positions in the East and to squeeze out its competitors.

The Latin occupation of Byzantium didn't last long. In 1261 Michael Paleologus reconquered Constantinople without difficulty, though he failed to bring it back to life. As Charles Diehl, a well-known

Salonika – St. Demetrius, mosaic, 7th century ▶

authority on Byzantium, remarks, in the meantime the empire had become "a shrunken body, weak and pitiful, with an enormous head: Constantinople." The death agonies of this swollen-headed monstrosity lasted for two long centuries. And once more religious struggles hastened its end: the conflict between Church and State.

Perhaps it would have been possible to save Constantinople by skilful diplomacy and a conciliatory attitude towards the Pope. But the Church was unwilling to show the slightest understanding. The ascetic spirit triumphed at the expense of a rational policy of rapprochement with Rome. Monks laid down the law: the era of the

Fresco, Mount Athos

Paleologues was marked by the great prosperity of the monasteries, both those on Mount Athos and elsewhere.

But it is an ill wind that blows no one any good: from that same era date those great Byzantine masterpieces of fresco and mosaic. The 13th, 14th and 15th centuries (often called "the renaissance of the Paleologues") have given us the beautiful creations of Mistra, of Mount Athos and of Salonika. As though by chance, they were built outside the capital. Administrative decentralisation extended to the arts, as if life were slowly receding from Constantinople.

Now it was the turn of the Turks, who swept forward to give the knock-out blow. At the end of the 13th century they had been organised into a powerful state by Osman or Othman, the founder of the

Ottoman dynasty. And they advanced rapidly, before long overrunning Serbia and Bulgaria. The bloody defeat inflicted in 1402 by Tamerlane's Mongols on Sultan Bajazet at Ankara, put a temporary stop to their plundering.

But twenty years later the Turks again went over to the attack. For the Byzantine emperors this was a humiliating and dramatic moment. Manuel II appealed for help to all the courts of Europe. At the Council of Florence, in 1439, John VIII went so far as to submit the Orthodox Church to the authority of the Pope. It was no use. A first tightening of the vice by Sultan Mohammed II cut communications between Byzantium and the Black Sea; a second squeeze, those with the Peloponnesus. In April 1453 the capital was besieged. Soon afterwards the Turkish conquest of Greece was completed, and on the 29th May, 1453, after two months of heroic resistance, Constantinople was taken by assault. *"Is there no Christian to receive my head?"* cried Constantine, the last of the Paleologues, defending the Gate of St. Romanus.

Modern times

The administrative decentralisation of Byzantium in and after the 11th century furthered both the advance of the Turks and the fall of the Empire. But also, in strengthening the power of the local lords, it created conditions for the rise of modern states and nations beneath the enormous black umbrella of the Turkish occupation of the Balkans. The whole evolution of modern Greece and of its Balkan neighbours should be seen in terms of this slow growth of local power.

After the fall of Constantinople the conquered part of Europe formed an administrative unit under the name of "Roumelia" (Roman land). Today this name refers only to that part of Greece which extends from Thessaly to the Gulf of Corinth. For long Turks and Venetians disputed over the island of Crete, which was finally occupied by the Turks in 1699. The Ionian Islands remained in Venetian hands till 1815, when they passed under British control.

Thus began those long, dark ages of bondage which still linger on in the unconscious of all that constitutes modern Greece. Islamic law makes but one distinction between peoples – that of religion. So the Patriarch became the "ethnarch" (= head of the people) and the Orthodox Church before long took on the character of a theocratic regime in which temporal and spiritual power were fused.

However, though recognising the privileges of the Church and its relative autonomy, the Turks had not abandoned the aim of converting the *rajas* (= slaves) to Islam. To that end they created the Janissary corps, the most redoubtable force of the Ottoman army, which was recruited from amongst Christian children of six to fifteen years old. In the same co-operative spirit they entrusted the maintenance of order to the *armatoloi*, that is to say a militia composed of Christians.

These met with resistance from the *kleftes* (= brigands), partisans of the maquis, filled with love of the mountains, of lamb à la pallikare [1] and of that typically Greek *levedia* which signifies at the same time generosity, courage, beauty and a thousand other things. They originated the "fustanella", the little pleated skirt which so amuses tourists in search of local colour, and the national costume in general: that of the evzone. It consists, apart from the skirt already mentioned, of white stockings like those of a ballerina, Turkish slippers, and a kind of skull-cap (*fessi*) worn on the back of the head and ending in a long bunch of tassels. These kleftes, too, are the source of the most beautiful folk songs. Moreover, later on they were the ones to bear the brunt of the War of Independence.

Slowly but surely we are getting to that celebrated war. Factors of the most varied origin contributed to it.

First: Those centuries of bondage saw the simultaneous rise of a neo-Hellenic bourgeoisie. Bold seafarers and cunning merchants, the Greeks ousted the Turks from these spheres, and their social evolution brought political emancipation in its train.

Next, the expansionist policy of Peter the Great and Catherine II, which aimed at the destruction of the Ottoman Empire, automatically favoured the cause of Greek independence. In other words, Greece became one of the pawns in the famous "Eastern Question" which throughout the 19th century was not only a most confused business but also an extremely explosive one. It was a question which preoccupied the Western powers above all: what was to become of Turkey, especially of Turkey in Europe? Russia desired its dismemberment, which no doubt would be greatly to its own benefit; but for that very reason Britain and Metternich's Austria desired the Ottoman

[1] Lamb roasted on a spit. *Pallikares* (= young men) refers to the guerrillas who in 1821 drove the Turks out of Greece.

Empire to remain intact and they indirectly obstructed the cause of Greek independence.

Finally, there was a third factor which prepared the ground for the revolt: the ideas of the French Revolution which spread to Greece through the medium of refugee intellectuals. The Declaration of Human Rights roused the spirits, kept hope alive and fanned the flames. In short, from the 18th century onward all necessary preconditions for the War of Independence were already there.

It broke out on March 25th 1821 – a national festival comparable to that of the 14th July in France – and it quickly spread throughout Greece. The blue and white flag flew over the country which had retrieved its own colours at last.

First, from 1821 to 1824, came a period of brilliant victories, e.g. that gained by Kolokotronis at Dervenakia (Peloponnesus) over Mahmoud Dramali. The names Diakos, Androutsos, Karaiskakis, Kanaris and Papaflessas, to mention only the most illustrious heroes, recall no less illustrious victories.

The second act lasted from 1825 to 1827. The play unfolded according to the rules of drama. The hero wrestled with his fate, then tragedy entered in the shape of Ibrahim Pasha of Egypt, who landed in Greece and whose armies sowed terror and death. The revolution was dying. To this phase of the war belong the famous "exodus" of Missolonghi and the death of Lord Byron.

But behold, the *catharsis* and the *deus ex machina* are near! In July 1827 the Triple Alliance (between Russia, Britain and France) was concluded. Each of these three powers had its particular reason for taking an interest in Greek independence. Russia in order to speed the disintegration of the Ottoman Empire; Britain to prevent Russia from annexing the territory liberated from the Turks; France for similar reasons. So they decided to mediate between Greece and Turkey and proposed that the latter should recognise the autonomy of Greece under the sovereignty of the Sultan. The refusal of the Porte (Turkish Government) to agree led to the naval battle of Navarino (20th October 1827) where the Turko-Egyptian fleet was annihilated.

Greece was free. The new country brimmed over with hope, and its people with good-will.

The third National Assembly (1827) had elected John Capodistria as president; however, he didn't last long. One Sunday morning, as he was coming out of Church, he was butchered by two members of the ancient Peloponnesian family of Mavromichali. In 1833 Prince Otto of Bavaria, imposed as the first king of Greece by the protector states Russia, France and Britain, disembarked at Nauplia. Spare the rod and spoil the child, they reasoned no doubt; paying attention

Assassination of John Capodistria

neither to the susceptibilities of the leaders nor to those of the populace, they used King Otto and his court to establish a truly alien rule. Greek independence thus started under the worst possible auspices, and as with people, the early experiences of nations are said to weigh heavily on their adult life.

A coup d'état on the night of the 2nd/3rd of September 1843 forced Otto to summon a National Assembly, which drew up the first Greek constitution. But constitutional monarchy did not bring the hoped-for political changes. And so another insurrection politely asked Otto to go home.

Britain started looking for a new Greek monarch. Its choice fell on the Danish Prince Wilhelm Georg of Glucksburg, who ascended the throne under the title of George the First, King of the Hellenes (October 1863). He had the happy thought of granting a new con-

Otto of Bavaria promising the constitution of 1843

stitution, which was voted in 1864 and which inaugurated parliamentary life in Greece. As for Britain, for once it managed to do the right thing; it gave the new king a dowry: the Ionian Islands, which were ceded to Greece also in 1864.

In the meantime, encouraged by Russian diplomacy, the "Grand Design" was gaining ground – a kind of utopian Greek expansionism which has been an ever present factor in modern Hellenism. So, after the Russo-Turkish war of 1877—1878, Turkey had to cede Thessaly to Greece. But not for long. The unfortunate Greek-Turkish war of 1897, which was as wounding to Greek national pride as the war of 1870 to the French, pushed the frontiers back again to the Lamia line, south of Thessaly.

It was a hard blow. Even today the memory of '97 still smarts. So it is understandable that the humiliated Greeks had but one thought:

revenge. They did not have to wait long for an opportunity; it came in the shape of an inter-Balkan alliance (between Serbia, Bulgaria and Greece) against Turkey. There was an excellent pretext for this: Turkey oppressed the Christian peoples on its European territory without distinction of nationality. But the real reason for this Balkan grouping lay deeper.

Let's follow closely these Machiavellian labyrinths of Greek history, for they explain how it was that this still inexperienced people sometimes lacked the adroitness needed to thwart the stratagems of older, more experienced diplomacies. We have now reached the eve of the First World War. A new factor entered into the Eastern question: Prussian Germany, whose *Drang nach Osten* passed through Macedonia. This new circumstance brought about a complete revision of British policy. No longer having the slightest interest in the preservation of the Turkish empire (which would have been in league with a powerful and Turkophile Germany), Britain openly encouraged Greek foreign policy and the Balkan Alliance. With the result that the wars of 1912—1913 against Turkey and subsequently against Bulgaria brought Greece portions of Crete, Eastern Macedonia and

WHO IS THE KING OF THE CASTLE?

January 1913 – the Tzar of Bulgaria after the conquest of Macedonia

Southern Epirus. With these, Eleutherios Venizelos, a young lawyer from Crete, made his entry into the political life of the country.

These wars were the prelude to the First World War. The Balkan Alliance fell apart. Serbia ranged itself alongside the Entente, Bulgaria sided with the Germans. Greece hesitated. King Constantine, brother-in-law of Kaiser Wilhelm and husband of Queen Sophia of the bejewelled *décolleté,* naturally sympathised with the Germans – that is to say he favoured Greek neutrality. The republican opposition led by Venizelos insisted on support of the Entente and a declaration of war. Eventually the Entente carried the day and, by way of precaution, blockaded Greece. King Constantine abdicated and was succeeded by his son Alexander. At the eleventh hour, in September 1917, Greece declared war.

Against this background occurred the debacle in Asia Minor, in 1922. Greece had to pay the price for King Constantine's pro-Germanism, for naturally the Allies felt rather lukewarm towards such a tardy ally.

The case was as follows: the treaty of Sèvres (August 1920) had, amongst other things, entrusted Greece with the administration of

August 1913 – King Constantine after the reconquest of Macedonia

1913 – The poet Matsoukas addressing the soldiers

the Smyrna region in Asia Minor. But the dynamic Mustapha Kemal repudiated the treaty. So it had to be enforced by military means; Greek troops landed in Ionia. On top of this came the elections of 1920. They have become a notable occasion in Greek history; and no wonder. On the heels of the diplomatic triumph of Venizelos, the staunch friend of the Entente, and at the very moment when the old expansionist dreams of the Greeks were about to be realised, this capricious people gave a majority vote, and therewith power, to the Royalists who fetched back King Constantine. Immediately Britain, which had always distrusted this pro-German king, withdrew its support. France, having openly supported Mustapha Kemal in order to counterbalance British influence in the Middle East, now also dropped its tardy ally. So single-handed Greece was left to carry the burden of an adventure in Asia Minor which before long, in 1922, turned into a disaster. In the end the coastal strip had to be evacuated and thousands of refugees – nearly a quarter of the population – flocked to the mother country.

In 1924 the Republic was proclaimed. It bloomed like a rose and faded before coming of age. On August 4th, 1936, General Metaxas' coup d'état brought totalitarianism to Greece. We will deal with this later.

On October 28th, 1940, Mussolini's ultimatum to Greece was rejected. The Italians invaded the country at a time when, after a year of "phony war", Britain had to bear the brunt of German aggression alone. Yet frostbitten soldiers, living skeletons clad in rags, pushed their pink and perfumed enemy back well beyond the frontiers.

But on April 6th 1941 (no April was ever like it), the Germans, having broken Yugoslav resistance, attacked in their turn. The war lasted three weeks, three weeks of incessant bombing, of furious resistance. One Sunday morning Hitler's armoured divisions paraded through an Athens where every window was closed and shuttered.

Thus began the occupation, the famine, the nameless tragedy. What can words avail? By 1942 births had fallen by half, whereas mortality had increased more than threefold. The war reduced the Greek population by 600,000 souls, more or less 10 %... Every morning throughout the terrible winter of 1941—1942 trucks collected the corpses of those who had died in the streets from starvation and cold.

On September 27th, 1941, that is a few months after the occupation, the National Liberation Front was set up, the political resistance movement whose military core was ELAS (initials for: *Ethnikos Laikos Apeleutherotikos Stratos* = National Popular Army of Liberation). After a short period of confusion and effusions, there could be no doubt that the nucleus of these organisations was unquestionably Communist. For this reason the parties of the Right, whose leaders were in London with King George II, formed as counterweights the EDES and EKKA resistance groups.

So before long a war on two fronts was being waged in the Greek mountains, and from then on it was possible to foresee what was to become known as the bloody December of 1944.

On October 12th 1944 Greece was liberated. The members of the EAM *(Ethniko Apeleftherotiko Metopo*, i.e. National Liberation Front) and the ELAS paraded in the streets of Athens, with clenched fists, shouting slogans and singing revolutionary songs. The air was heavy with events impending. General Scobie, the commander of the British troops which had landed in Greece, ordered the ELAS forces to disarm. The Ministers of the Left, who had taken part in the government of "Unity", resigned. Supporters of ELAS held a tremendous protest demonstration. The police opened fire on the demonstrators - and those were the first shots of the civil war. One might say, with Thucydides, that "*this day would be the beginning of great misfortunes to the Hellenes.*" [1] For forty days there raged a

1944 – Greek partisans and a British soldier

frenzy of blood and death. Officially this carnage was ended by the agreement of Varkiza (February 12th, 1945). But terror is a drug and its habit not easily thrown off.

In 1946 a plebiscite brought back King George II of Glucksburg. Civil war broke out anew, this time on an organised scale. The partisans of ELAS once more took to the mountains. But Britain, in its superior wisdom, renounced its role as a Great Power. In 1947 it declared itself no longer able to cope with (i.e. to finance) the situation in Greece. No matter: with a grand gesture the United States, those universal bankers, took over. Civil war, terror, reprisals and counter-reprisals grew in intensity.

Yet a year later the civil war came to an end, for many reasons, but partly at least because of the schism between Tito and Moscow. The Yugoslav frontiers were closed to partisans obeying the Stalinist slogans. That sealed the fate of the Greek Left.

The elections of 1952 – the electoral period is four years, but this is rarely adhered to – gave power to Marshal Papagos, the leader of the "National Union", an organisation of the extreme Right. The

[1] Thucydides, *The History of the Peloponnesian War*, p. 81.

Communist party led only a clandestine existence, if it can be called that. The Socialist party was scattered to the four winds – that is to say to the various Liberal parties, of which there was a surfeit. They didn't manage to form an opposition block, and it was on that lack of cohesion that Papagos' Union correctly banked. In fact, in the general election of February 19th, 1956, this National Union party, then led by the Marshal's successor Karamanlis, obtained an admittedly small majority over the anti-governmental coalition. This was slightly increased in the 1958 elections when the E.D.A., the extreme left wing party, emerged as the leading party in opposition.

The Cyprus question now came to the fore. Demonstrations and scuffles multiplied. In spite of – or because of – Britain's reintroduction of whipping and other punitive "measures" into the island, Greece threatened to leave the Atlantic Community, which caused it too much loss of blood and too many humiliations.

In February 1959 an agreement, a masterpiece of compromise, was signed between Greece, Turkey and Britain, whereby Cyprus was to become a republic with a Greek-Cypriot president (Archbishop Makarios was elected) and a Turkish-Cypriot vice-president, and Britain was to retain her military bases, with her sovereignty, in two small areas of the island.

THE DIADOCHS

ATTIKON

To be or not to be

This is what is always happening to me in Italy; in France, too, though in a different way.

— *Italiana?*

— *No.*

— *Spagnole?*

— No.

— *Egiziana?*

— *No.*

— *Portughese?*

— *No.*

At *Cinese* in order to be left in peace, I say yes. Why the devil does it never occur to anybody that I might be Greek? Surely this seems unlikely to most people because they never freely associate the present shape of Southern Europe with ancient Greece. Why does the word "Greek" have one meaning in school books, and quite another in real life?

This is a question which often disturbs me, for it runs counter not only to what I have been taught at school, but to all that the average Greek gets rammed into him from morning to night. He is the heir of the ancients and can prove it to you up to the hilt. Didn't they live on politics and plain water? Well, he does practically the same. They rushed into civil war at the slightest provocation; their offspring preserve this noble tradition to the best of their ability. Xenios Zeus (patron of strangers) is still the Greek god par excellence, and all the hearths are wide open to welcome strangers. As to philosophy, looked at more closely what does it come down to? Palavers in cafes, and that is exactly the main occupation of the diadochs (successors). How they can argue! Stretched out on two chairs in the sun the modern Hellenes, between two Turkish coffees, contemptuously spurn

To be or not to be

Julius Caesar's stern admonition: *"How often will the glory of your ancestors preserve you from the consequences of your own mistakes?"*

To be or not to be Greek? This question has confronted the descendants of Homer fairly late in the day. Up to the 19th century they were Greek without knowing it. But in the course of that interminable, nouveau-riche and suspicious 19th century the racial purity of the Hellenes was called in question. Man has been called a thinking reed. In this particular instance however he proved to be a somewhat swollen reed, to wit: Herr Doktor J. P. Fallmerayer who, basing his argument on the repeated Slav invasions of Greece from the 7th century on, evolved a theory that the Greek element had been completely obliterated (*History of the Morea in the Middle Ages, The Albanian Element in Greece,* etc.). This happened halfway through the last century, that is to say just after Greek independence had been won at the cost of a long and difficult war. One can well imagine what kind of reception this bright idea met with in the land of the gods. It called forth an avalanche of pamphlets, counter-attacks, lucid or inflammatory treatises; Constantine Paparrigopoulos took upon himself the task of refuting Fallmerayer in his *History of the Hellenic Nation,* in six volumes, which even today is the only comprehensive work on the history of Greece.

After Hitler's gas chambers it would be easy to demolish this whole argument with a stroke of the pen by simply pointing to the striking parallel with Nazi anti-semitism. But the "objective" historian watches us at every turn, ready to accuse us of a "flight into the sociological". So we have to take up the debate on the same level at which it is presented to us.

Let's take a closer look. What is the meaning of that abstract concept of "race"? In the last resort it is but one of the numerous prejudices of that 19th-century circle which discovered materialism and was dazzled by it; a materialism for which, by the way, Marx had no use. Fallmerayer himself associated with the German Left of 1848. So it is in the name of a prejudice that "races" have been identified purely and simply with peoples and their histories. And if one prejudice deserves another, one might just as well oppose it with that fetish of the 20th century: language. For even if one admitted the "slavisation" of Greece, a fundamental difference would remain between the Russian-speaking Slavs along the banks of the Volga and the Slav who is born in Athens, speaks Greek and learns that Greek history is his own. This is precisely what a contemporary specialist, Antoine Bon, maintains when he writes about the veracity of historical and archeological documents: "Even if at one time the foreign element was numerically stronger, as seems indicated by the abundance of Slav place-names which were more numerous in medieval times than nowadays, it was from the 8th century onwards cut off from its country of origin and its fellows of the same race. Thus it could not but submit to the influence of the Greeks whose civilisation was incomparably higher and who could count on the help of an Empire of considerable political and military power. Thus the Slav tribes seemed to disappear, to vanish, assimilated by the Greeks whom they had at one time driven back and threatened: they adopted the language, the religion of the country. This absorption did not occur as quickly as is sometimes thought: it required several military expeditions in 783, at the beginning of the 9th century, and again under Michael III, to re-establish Imperial authority; in the 10th century some tribes once more rebelled, maintaining their ethnic character quite distinctly until the 13th century and not losing or forgetting it definitely until the 15th. But the assimilation was so complete and final that some historians have been led to deny that there had ever been Slavs in the Peloponnesus, or at any rate that there had been many, an assertion which at first sight might appear legitimate, but which would fail to explain all the anomalies observed in the course of the 7th and 8th centuries and the changes in the country which became evident from the 9th century onward."

If to the Slav element one adds the Turkish and Frankish mixtures, the racial purity of the Hellenes becomes even more problematic. But there still remains the unity of language to associate the diadochs with the fame of their ancestors.

Logos

Æsop the slave was not only a writer of fables, at times he also enacted them, as for example in the well known dispute between his master and himself about language. An ancient Greek would have had no doubt as to the reason why language is one of the most precious things in the world. A modern Greek, on the other hand, has more occasion to be critical of its shortcomings. The drama – Greeks bashfully call it "the question" – of language which he has witnessed during the past century may not be unique (it would seem that the Arabs are up against a similar situation); it is nonetheless a very exceptional case.

What is called "modern" Greek is in fact a plurality of languages; its diversity is crystallised in the contrast between *Demotic* and *Katharevoussa*.

Demotic (= common) is spoken by everybody; it is the literary and living language. Wits call it "hairy" *(malliari)* in memory of the long-haired intellectuals who struggled for its adoption.

Katharevoussa (purist) is the official language, the required language for all learned works. It is also used by newspapers, except those of the Left. This clearly shows the social role of each of these languages. Katharevoussa represents a spirit of conformism and reaction, for it addresses itself to the "literate", i.e. to those privileged few who can afford to attend secondary schools. The less exclusive Demotic is understood by everybody and for that very reason constitutes a progressive factor. So much so, that authors of scientific works written in Demotic are often taxed with subversive opinions – with all that that entails . . .

At which precise moment did this divergence begin? Impossible to say. A linguistic dualism can be noted throughout the Byzantine period; it continued under Turkish occupation. But not until the 19th century did it grow into a veritable Babel. *Babylon*, in fact, is the title of a comedy by Byzantios, a 19th-century author, in which the differences between the various Greek idioms give rise to a whole lot of farcical misunderstandings. Thenceforth the struggle for Demotic entered its epic stage. An attempt to translate the Gospels into the language of the common people unleashed a revolt in a country never at a loss to find something to squabble about anyway. Whole generations pride themselves on the heroic struggles which resulted in final victory for Demotic, at least in the literary field. Jean Psichari, French through adoption by Ernest Renan, headed the movement.

As to ancient Greek, I would say that the modern language is more closely related to it than, for example, Italian to Latin. What tends to create the opposite impression is the difference in pronunciation. A modern Greek pronounces Homeric verse in much the same way as he pronounces common swear words (of which he has an impressive number!). The classical scholar, that is to say the foreigner, splits his diphthongs. He says "pa-is" instead of "pess" (*pais* = child). To my mind that is one of the surest ways to murder Plato's divine language. I couldn't prove it, but neither can those who take the opposite view. The only possible arbiter, the tape-recorder, hadn't been invented at the time. I'd like to recommend the following as a substitute: listen to the same tragedy, *Oedipus Rex* for instance, in the "Erasmian" Greek of the scholars and in Greek Greek. Then we'll talk about it again. If you have an opportunity to do this in the theatre at Delphi or Epidaurus, so much the better.

In general, modern Greek has become increasingly degenerate when compared with the ancestral language. By largely maintaining the latter's syntax and grammar, Katharevoussa has kept closer to it than has Demotic; for one thing by resisting the infiltration of foreign words. On the other hand, what it thus gained in orthodoxy it lost in savour and quickness compared with Demotic. This closer affinity of Katharevoussa to ancient Greek has often led foreign friends of mine to declare themselves in favour of it: modern Greek texts would in this way become directly accessable to all who are familiar with ancient Greek. That's the same kind of argument which, when the drachm was devalued in 1953, made the foreigners shout with joy: Greece became the cheapest country in the world . . . for the tourists. An "interesting" country in the same way that a bargain is interesting.

To the Englishman or American who takes his language for granted all this may seem utterly absurd and futile. However it is nothing of the sort. For as you may remember, *logos* is the Greek word for two things: word and reason. "A question of language" therefore means a problem concerning reason, a human drama; and it is in these terms that one should measure the significance of the existing confusion. The absence of a word implies the absence of the concept for which it stands. Is it just coincidence that there is no exact equivalent in modern Greek for such modern concepts as "structure", "conjuncture", etc.? Such examples could be multiplied ad lib.; translators will bear me out. It all goes to show the double and ancient function of language, which makes any deficiency in expression indicative of a certain backwardness both in reasoning and in historical development.

This state of affairs is at least partly due to the pathological prolongation in Greece of the interminable Middle Ages which, suddenly and without transition, opened out in to modern times. The Byzantines presented the Renaissance to the Western peoples; in the East, its place remained empty. Thus there was an absence of intermediate connections and corresponding mental structures. We are touching the roots of the problem. Strictly speaking it should be possible, with a lot of effort and a little luck, to create a vocabulary, a language, a means of expression. But it is not possible to create a history out of the blue, from behind one's desk.

Paideia

It is not surprising in the circumstances that the whole educational system bears the imprint of this confusion. During his four years of (compulsory) primary schooling the Greek child learns a *different* grammar and a *different* spelling from those he is taught afterwards, in the "gymnasium" which corresponds to the English grammar school. With the result that after twelve years of study the pupil is definitely fed up with Greek letters and with the humanities. For to make his plight even worse, during his eight years at the grammar school he has also to spend one hour a day on ancient Greek. Starting with Xenophon he wades through Arion and the orators: Isocrates, Lysias and Demosthenes. After all that, for the sake of honour and the fatherland, he sweats bucketfuls over Homer. In comparison Plato seems to him but child's play. In the eighth and highest form (comparable with the English sixth form or American senior high-school class) the final and most difficult test awaits him before he can enter Paradise: the Tragedies, Euripides or Sophocles. On finishing grammar school, the youngster has been taught no philosophy apart from a little elementary logic and psychology. He has only an inkling of mathematics and science. In short, his intellectual equipment is pretty lightweight.

Anyway, he (or she) has by now his *apolytirion* (roughly equivalent to the English General Certificate of Education at A Level; or an American high-school diploma). What does it lead to? In the first place to those posts in banks, government departments and such-like with which the all-important bourgeoisie feather their nests. Or, in the case of a girl, to marriage; so much the better if she has a smattering of English or French. Those who can afford to go to college – fees are extremely high – have the choice between two universities: that of Salonika, which has a reputation of being progressive because it employs professors who are in favour of Demotic, and that of Athens which was founded in 1837. To be admitted, they have to pass all over again the same exam they took three months before. Why this duplication? No one knows. That is the kind of question one should not ask.

The faculty which attracts most students is that of Law. Figures for 1938 show that 45 % of the university graduates were lawyers and 33 % doctors. Of course it's not the poetry of the Civil Code (introduced in 1945 to replace Roman law) which attracts these youngsters. Their main concern is how best to earn their living. And law opens all doors: to the diplomatic service, to the bar, to politics, to a large dowry and even, should the occasion arise, to poetry or music.

The average period at university is four years. So a university degree in Greece rates about the same as a university degree in Britain or America, but provides no safeguard at all against unemployment.

The self-denial and disinterestedness of those who devote themselves to university careers border on the angelic. Having taken their degree, they have to write a doctoral thesis which is more or less the equivalent of the German doctorate as it takes much longer than the British Ph.D. The title thus obtained is "academic" in a double sense; for in order to qualify for employment at an institution of higher education, the young doctor – who is by now in his forties – has to pass what the Germans call a "habilitation" thesis (the *Yphigessia)*. He is then allowed to take on a course of lectures . . . without remuneration. He doesn't get paid until he is appointed to a regular professorship. This may happen, if all goes well, by the time he has reached his fifties. He then earns the equivalent of nearly £70 or $200 per month – admittedly in a country whose standard of life is lower than that of Britain. And all this on one indispensable condition: that he is not suspected of "subversive opinions". What is meant by that? . . . Impossible to know beforehand. One doesn't find that out until after the blow has fallen, when it is too late.

I was frightened, horribly frightened at school. Yet it was one of the best girls' schools in Athens. All my adult fears are childish compared to that terror of my infancy. The doors of the classrooms were fitted with little windows, rather like portholes, through which during lessons the headmistress used to pop her head and eye us – with two pairs of eyes, for she wore glasses. In the classroom itself a supervisor sat next to the teacher. We were the opposite of Mount Athos: in our school everyone belonged to the female sex, or rather to the third sex. The basis of our training was fear, just as in a concentration camp, and often each day I thought I would die. But at least it was a step forward that we weren't beaten, which was the regular practice in the boys' grammar schools.

One can therefore imagine with what feeling and hope I welcomed the recent progress in education in Greece. Montessori kindergartens, groups of psychologists and psychoanalysts undertaking the task of educating parents, and enlightened teachers who like their profession.

A village school

All these things, which are due entirely to private enterprise, belong to the post-war period and are as yet only rare. But they are enough to fill one with confidence in the future of this dark and obstinate people, thin as crickets – the neo-Hellenes.

Conversation with Henry Miller

"If you don't praise your house to the skies, it'll come tumbling about your ears," says a Greek proverb. What's more, it has to be done with conviction, which isn't always so easy. So when it comes to bestowing credit, I gladly give way to Henry Miller and his beautiful and generous *Colossus of Maroussi: "... But that conversation taught me immediately that the Greeks are an enthusiastic, curious-minded, passionate people.* Passion *– it was something I had long missed in France. Not only passion, but contradictoriness, confusion, chaos – all these sterling human qualities I rediscovered and cherished again in the person of my new-found friend.* And generosity. *I had almost thought it had perished from the earth. There we were, a Greek and an American, with something in common, yet two vastly different beings. It was a splendid introduction to that world which was about to open before my eyes. I was already enamoured of Greece, and the Greeks, before catching sight of the country. I could see in advance that they were a friendly, hospitable people, easy to reach, easy to deal with."*

Dear Henry Miller, if I told you that I have rarely met such deep emotion, such justice and such vibrating sensuality in a foreigner's reactions to Greece, that I thank you from the bottom of my heart for having so eagerly embraced this harsh and thirsty soil, our score in this battle of flowers would be about even.

However, you know us ... You know how prone we are to argue, to cavil. So you won't be surprised if I tell you that I don't feel quite comfortable in this Paradise you conjure up; if I were an art critic, I would point out the want of plastic values, of dissonances in your

◀ After the earthquake

picture. You use nothing but perfectly harmonious colours. You dislike sharp contrasts, foils; and that is exactly what I would now like to supply. Everything enchants you in our country, even our poverty, even our bare feet and our numerous faults. You go even further: you like us because of them.

"I love Greece for its light and poverty," you write, and that is very typical of you. Does that mean that if one or the other of these aspects were to vanish . . . you would be less fond of us? What a curious, abstract form your love takes. Like so many others with whom otherwise you have nothing in common (I refer to those typically bourgeois people who are always thrilled by scandalous economic conditions), you have been taken in by that legendary Greek frugality which makes the majority of people content to feed on bricks and pure air. Do you really think that, if he could keep warm, the Greek peasant would be less friendly and less hospitable? In a book on Sweden, Bastide poses the problem of the high suicide statistics of that prosperous country: *"Are some diseases born of good fortune, and how can they be overcome?"* he asks. Your attitude, which judges misery in terms of aesthetics, seems to me the exact counterpart of those diseases of good fortune. Finally, you have a lot in common with the ancient Medusa: you both suck the life out of people – she, to turn them into stones, you to turn them into aesthetic objects. You even preach them a sermon and prove to them that this is the height of happiness: poor but honest – in other words aesthetic. At least that is what I take you to mean when you say:

" 'Yes,' I said, 'I'm crazy enough to believe that the happiest man on earth is the man with the fewest needs. And I also believe that if you have light, such as you have here, all ugliness is obliterated. Since I've come to your country I know that light is holy: Greece is a holy land to me.'

" 'But have you seen how poor the people are, how wretchedly they live?'

" 'I've seen worse wretchedness in America', I said. 'Poverty alone doesn't make people wretched.' "

You would admit however that poverty alone does not make them happy, either. Occasionally it might even aggravate their wretchedness. Why then do you insist on it? And why are you so hard on that unfortunate American Greek (we call such as he *Brouklis,* those typical Greeks from Brooklyn, somewhat naive and, in the eyes of their countryman at any rate, rolling in money) who, having tasted the material welfare of the New World, could not help comparing it with his native country and finding the latter backward?

I think I understand the reason for this extreme romanticism: it's the fear that certain values might get lost, values which mean a lot to you (and no less to us, I assure you), such as: love, friendship, generosity, affection, pride, and that endurance which according to you can be produced only by suffering, as a pearl by an oyster. You attribute to contemporary Greece a similar Vestal mission to the one it fulfilled in the past. Similar, also, to that of the Negroes in the world of today – as you have written in so many words. For you have your own ideas as to what is or is not Greek. *"The ancient Greek was a murderer,"* you write, *"he lived amidst brutal clarities which tormented and maddened the spirit. He was at war with everyone, including himself. Out of this fiery anarchy came the lucid, healing metaphysical speculations which even to-day enthrall the world."* And so it is with the best of intentions that you want to keep Greece sheltered from civilisation and modern technique.

You have touched on a serious problem here, in some ways "the" problem not only of our small country, but of the world of today. But having posed the problem, you are content to leave it at that. What seems to you a solution, in effect doesn't solve anything. I'm well aware that the turn history is about to take is dangerous enough; but all you do is to attempt to check its course. Yet we won't be able to control that course by ignoring technique and modern civilisation, but only by making use of them. The best way to combat the monsters conjured up by the modern Sorcerer's Apprentice is not to flee from them, but to stand up to them. In the end such childish flight destroys the very values it pretends to defend. If the emotions are to reach full maturity they require, who would deny it, a steady temperature, a steady social climate. Below a certain standard of living and technical equipment they become blighted. The history of Greece over the last twenty years provides the most spectacular confirmation of this.

Another detail: those aspects that are so dear to you and which you ascribe to "authentic" Greece are often nothing but Turkish relics which we would have done much better to get rid of. At the risk of appearing pedantic, may I remind you that Aristotle in his *Nicomachean Ethics* has defined virtue as "the golden mean" *(messotis)*, which seems to me an excellent definition of the ancient Greek world and its basic principles. Frankly, do you think it could be applied to contemporary Greece, where everything is excessive? That generosity which delighted you so much often turns to waste, a squandering of nerves, of ideas thrown on paper any old how, of love, blood, time, everything. Mind you, that *libido* which permeates all life in Greece and which maintains an emotional temperature of 110 degrees in the shade, is precious. So is that all-pervading eroticism, aggressive and perpetually unsatiated; and that bottomless melancholy: a black beast nurtured in everybody's heart. But what of the counterpart of all this – the immoderation, the *hubris* (insolence)? Those hideous crimes for the sake of so-called "honour", those sisters butchered by their brothers for having yielded to the man they loved? And that touchiness and conceit, so easily offended that daggers and knives are drawn at the slightest provocation, and brawls in taverns about the most trivial misunderstandings turned into Shakespearian tragedies? To tell you the truth – if the ancient Greek personified the Aristotelian ideal of moderation, the modern Greek seems to me the nearest approach to Romantic extravagance. As you have expressed it so well – and I fully agree – in a certain sense nowadays such intemperance is the only proper reaction; for beneath the distorted mask of madness it tries to rediscover the "authentic" face of man. But once again, one should not stress this too much – which means to say that once more moderation has the last word.

However, all this is still of rather secondary importance and has not touched the root of our differences. I've reached that now. I have even found a nice and impressive word for it: "engagement", or rather, the opposite. Let me explain. You lived about a year in Greece, in 1939, when the Metaxas dictatorship was at its height. That dictatorship is largely to be blamed for the present bad state of our country. You had no eyes for that aspect of Greece. I haven't much use for the sort of bad conscience which is fashionable nowadays but which often smacks of phariseeism and does no one any good. But neither do I care for the blissful innocence exemplified by Marie Antoinette and her cake. To you, the sky seemed always blue. Yet at that particular time it was full of bad omens. You weren't aware of that crack in it which was about to widen till the heavens were torn apart. You didn't notice the ominous rumble heralding the coming a few years later of the civil war, with all its insanity and fratricide. And those menacing clouds which shrouded the light escaped your attention too. You managed to climb all the 999 steps of the fortress of Nauplia without hearing the groans rising from its dungeons – the very dungeons into which Kolokotronis, the hero of the War of Independence, was thrown. Yet in 1939 they were full of Communists. Today they are empty, sure enough. Their inmates are now elsewhere.

I am a typical child of my age. I assure you it gave me quite a shock to see tractors move about in the fields once peace had come again – though a very relative peace, for I know how difficult it is to work and live on the land in this country of ours.

So you see, I can't entirely prevent myself from praising it after all. As you have put it so well, à propos of Seferis, our T. S. Eliot: *"He* (the Greek expatriate) *is passionate about his own country, his own people, not in a hidebound,* chauvinistic *way but as a result of patient discovery following upon years of absence abroad. This passion for one's country is a special peculiarity of the intellectual Greek who has lived abroad. In other peoples I have found it distasteful, but in the Greek I find it justifiable, and not only justifiable, but thrilling, inspiring."*

I'll take advantage of your understanding to allow myself one final eulogy – not a mean one at that. Twenty years have passed since your journey in Greece. Quite a long time in these atomic and explosive days . . . A lot of water has flowed under the bridges. And blood. But how proud I am to be able to say that there is no trace whatsoever of anti-semitism in Greece nowadays. It's not that people have taken a conscious stand against it, nor is it a matter of considered behaviour. Physiology and anatomy have more to do with it than morals. It results from a constitutional inability to grasp what is meant by racial conflicts within the human species. On the other hand every Greek finds it difficult to conceive that this same human species may not always be violently divided on political issues. He is well informed about world politics; he has very decided views on all international problems, he has an economic programme, a war strategy, a diplomacy, he is ripe for the premiership. Greece has as many statesmen as it has inhabitants: seven million in all. There is a true story, passed on from one generation to the next, which is a good illustration of this eminently neo-Hellenic trait: In 1904, during the Russo—Japanese war, a newspaper appeared in Athens sonorously entitled: "FORWARD!" In true neo-Greek fashion its editor followed the various phases of the war day by day in scintillating articles, in which he developed his own strategy at length. One day he even published an article under the peremptory headline: "*Further to the right, Kuropatkin!*" and proceeded to give the Russian general, in Greek, very pertinent advice as to the tactics to be applied, the route to be followed, etc. Just afterwards came the Russian defeat at Mukden. Next day, the paper's editorial started: "*We warned you, general Kuropatkin, but you chose not to listen . . .*"

And now after all I feel rather guilty at having met your generous praise with so many reproaches. Let us make peace. With the help of the language of figures, which has a poetry of its own, we may perhaps be able to settle our accounts.

"Before the war, the national income of Greece per inhabitant was already lower than anywhere else in Europe. The subsequent ravages wrought by war, enemy occupation and the prolonged guerilla struggles have inflicted losses on this country greater than those suffered by any other country involved."

It was not just in the hope of extracting maximum aid under the Marshall Plan that the Memorandum of the Greek delegation to the O.E.E.C. in 1948 started off on this sober note. For once reality was so grim that there was no need to touch it up, as is sometimes done.

The reality of Greek poverty stands out even more if one compares the average Greek income per head with that of other countries. In 1939 the situation was as follows:

Country	*Income per inhabitant, in U.S. dollars*
Great Britain	486.2
France	361.7
Greece	78.9

How is this money income to be translated into real terms, what is its purchasing power? According to the results of an inquiry into a sample 500 working-class families undertaken by the American mission in Greece (February—May 1948), the composition of 10,000 recorded meals was as follows: 13% consisted mainly of fish, less than 10% of meat, 27% of nothing but vegetables, 16% of potatoes, 14% of pasta (macaroni etc.), 11% of green vegetables. The majority of working-class families had only one meal a day.

At first sight one might think that the condition of the working class is not decisive in a country where, in 1917, the chief industries employed no more than 35,000 workers. By 1931 the total number of workers had increased to 242,000; and it has doubled since. But that is still not nearly enough to create an industrial working class in the Western sense. So let's take a look at other sections of the population. In October 1946 the salaries of civil servants as well as other clerical employees would enable a family of two to buy per day: three rations of bread, four tram tickets, half a bottle of milk, less than six ounces of oil, 5½ lbs of potatoes, and a little water, light and fuel.

The condition of the peasants is hardly any better, and that is especially serious in a country where 60 % of the population live on the land, in other words in a predominantly agrarian country. The most important agricultural areas are around Patras and Corinth, where wine and raisins are produced; the plain of Thessaly which is rich in cereals; Thrace and Macedonia where tobacco is grown; and the oil-producing districts of Mytilaena and Calamate. The industrial centres are Athens, the Piraeus, Salonika, Volos and Kavala.

Only 25 % of the total surface of Greece is cultivated and it is not easy to add substantially to that meagre percentage: mountains and rocks cover a large part of the territory. That's why the Greek peasant emigrates so easily, preferably to the United States. Sometimes he comes back, with his savings; in which case he often starts an hotel in the village of his birth. His hotel is provided with all comforts, and he welcomes you in a Yankee accent. More often he stays in New York. He never manages to adapt himself completely, and you will meet him of an evening when, homesick and blue, you are looking for a Greek restaurant. In view of the balance of payments, which is constantly at a deficit, these emigrants are very valuable. Like the good Greeks they are, they have a strong sense of family solidarity. So once a month they send money orders to their families, in dollars of course, which amount to a nice little annual sum in foreign exchange without any counterbalancing item. For this reason the grateful fatherland declared 1951 "Homecoming Year", in the hope of touching these hearts of gold and enticing them home for a few weeks.

The main agricultural products are tobacco, raisins and, in the past few years, cotton and rice also. Tobacco is the trump card in foreign trade, for it takes up 50.41 % of all exports and thus enables the Greek worker to eat bread; for 42 % of wheat consumption is covered by imports.

Not a very bright picture, to be sure; but not quite desperate either. It may even improve. Mechanisation of agriculture for example, water control, irrigation, drainage, etc. could raise agricultural output. According to the estimate of the U.N. Food and Agricultural Organisation one might justifiably expect an increase in output of 100 to 200 %. The cattle-raising which such improvements would make possible would enable the peasant to adopt a standard of living higher than the present extremely frugal one, and would at the same time increase his purchasing power, thus creating a greater demand for industrial products.

Should that demand be satisfied – here we touch on the central problem of political economy – and should further industrialisation be encouraged? Or would it be better to develop agriculture? And what do each of these alternatives mean politically? That an ex-

clusively agricultural economy, with its constant threat of bad harvests, is undesirable, no one would deny. Fr m the outset the Greek delegation to the O.E.E.C. declared: "For the country's recovery the maximum development of agriculture and fisheries will be required, but the main need is for industrialisation". This implies making better use of waterfalls and a decentralisation of industry which would also solve the problem of overpopulation in the towns. So when Marshall aid was distributed, nearly one third was allocated to industrial and hydro-electric projects (16 % to the former, 13 % to the latter).

All the same this beautiful programme came to naught for two reasons. In the first place an enormous sum of this American money

went on military expenditure (and continues to be swallowed up by it, though to a somewhat lesser degree). Since the Liberation, milliards of dollars in one form or another have found their way to Greece; yet reconstruction is quite disproportionate. The following table gives an approximate idea of military expenditures:

American aid to Greece since the Liberation
(in millions of dollars)

	Oct. 1944–June 1947	*June '47–July '48*	*'48–'49*	*'49–'50*
Economic	318	170.7	249.7	255.6
Military	14	172.0	170.7	142.0

No doubt this is nothing new; it's more or less the same the world over. Greece, however, is unique in the disproportion between the share of the total budget allocated to military purposes, and that put aside for economic reconstruction. A disproportion thought by some Greeks to be gratuitous, since in the present international situation they regard lightly the idea of any threat to Greece's frontiers. What's the odds: every economic programme is built on military bases . . .

A second – and equally unoriginal – factor which determines the volume of American aid and the use to which it is put, is Greece's position within the Atlantic Alliance. Tit for tat, and so Greece, like many other countries, in return for the economic assistance she receives allows American naval bases on her territory, grants extra-territorial status to American citizens, and cuts down her tobacco exports. In fact this noble product, which for so long has nourished Greek workers and peasants alike (maybe against economic common sense, but that is neither here nor there), is no longer able to stand up to the competition of American tobacco. It has become more and more difficult to find sufficient outlets for it. It's a matter of elementary logic, therefore, that the struggle should be abandoned. So far so good. But who profits from this disappearance of Greek tobacco from the markets? Not the Greek worker, surely. His fate is now determined by the laws governing American trade, which imposes its conditions on the world tobacco market by downright economic blackmail. Briefly, it's one of the many instances of "guided economy". Guided by whom? Essentially, by American credits. With an eye to what? To the sovereign good.

However, I'd like to tackle one or two backward prejudices about the backward state of Greece, which is not quite darkest Africa after all. That famous legend of the "unbelievable" Greek roads for example, which discourages so many car drivers. It is terribly dated. The main arterial roads are macadamised; the others are quite decent. Remember, by the way, that at the time of the Liberation barely 300 miles of passable road surface remained. Since then the whole network has been completely overhauled, and new roads are under construction. The present-day Athenian takes particular pride in the one which encircles Attica and, following the coastline of the Gulf of Saronicos, is to link Athens with Cape Sounion.

The railways have long been nationalised and, like British Railways, have been running at a loss. The Simplon-Orient express (run since 1920) undertakes to transport the traveller in three days and nights from Paris to Athens.

But why these diabolical vehicles in a country a quarter of whose territory consists of islands? You'd do much better to take a boat.

As a rule they don't keep to a fixed timetable, that is to say they are either 4 hours earlier or 4 hours later than the scheduled time. On the other hand they are ridiculously cheap. Moreover, how delightful are those departures from the Piraeus and those arrivals, next day, at one of the Cyclades. You are bound to travel in the company of poultry and other domestic animals, fluttering noisily inside their tied-up baskets. I must confess I've never been able to understand the amused surprise of tourists at these madly cackling fowls. What's so funny about the fact that an islander who goes to visit his shoemaker-cousin in Athens should, like any self-respecting Greek, bring a little present from his backyard?

Lastly, that supreme luxury – which isn't all that expensive if one carries foreign exchange – the plane. There is a daily service connecting Athens with Salonika, Rhodes and Crete; and other lines touch down at all the main towns in Greece, not to mention Belgrade, Istanbul, Cyprus and Alexandria.

Taxi fares are also ridiculously cheap, and in Athens you will be quite overcome by their splendour. Nothing but Buicks, Oldsmobiles, Cadillacs – enough to make you turn up your nose in disgust at the London taxis for the rest of your life, and even more elegant than New York's. What's more, there is no tipping.

"A little hovel is all we need," sang the miraculous choir of cripples in the film "Miracle in Milan". Their Greek brother completely agrees, for he hasn't even got a hut. There was a pressing housing shortage even before the war. In 1922, after the Asia Minor catastrophe, the influx of refugees brought the crisis to a head (one refugee to every 4 inhabitants . . .). On the morrow of the Liberation war damage in Greece proportionate to population surpassed that of all other countries in Europe: 216,000 families had been made homeless and the losses amounted to a total destruction of 23 % of all pre-war habitations and buildings. After the war against the Germans came the civil war. Earthquakes – first in 1953, on the Ionian Islands, next in the spring of 1954 in Thessaly – completed the catastrophe. And reconstruction takes a long time.

Yet Athens easily deceives the eye. Every day new buildings shoot up like mushrooms. Rents are frightfully high for an average budget, similarly purchase prices. They are, like all sums of any significance, calculated in gold sovereigns. For a medium-sized flat one should reckon on a monthly rent of about one gold sovereign, (about 65s. or $9 currently), per room. Whence comes this stream of gold sovereigns which flows through the wallets, pockets, tills and over the counters – a phenomenon apparently unique in Europe?

It's a well known fact that all that glisters is not gold. But in this case gold hardly enters into it. This craving for sovereigns is simply a symptom of people's aversion to the drachm. True, distrust and monetary instability have always been with us. But the giddy fall of the drachm between 1942 and 1944 brought this public phobia to a head. It resembled the inflation in the U.S.S.R. after the revolution of 1917, or that of the German mark after the first world war. This is how the monetary circulation affected the cost of living:

Index of the circulation and the cost of living from 1941—1944

	Notes	Cost of living
April 1941	1	1
October 1944	5,260,465	2,305,984,911

By the end of 1943, civil servants and other salaried employees were no longer paid by the month but every five days; for the drachm depreciated from week to week. Never has the famous vicious circle of wages and prices chased its tail like this. Office workers carried enormous napkins bulging with paper money around with them, milliards in banknotes – just enough to buy two cups of chicory coffee. Ever since, people's aversion to the drachm has been such that it will long outlast the circumstances that gave rise to it. To this day it is one of the major obstacles to economic recovery.

And one must admit events have justified this distrust. In April 1953 a new monetary devaluation made the dollar – which acts as standard for the drachm – go up from 15,000 to 30,000 drachms. This was of course a boon for all who happened to possess dollars or other foreign exchange. From one day to the next they saw their fortunes doubled. But what about those others, who lived on drachms, that is to say the large majority? They had to put up with yet another rise in prices. They decided they wouldn't be caught like that again and hastened to invest all their savings in gold sovereigns. But the tourists came in large numbers, and are still coming. It's an ill wind that blows no one any good.

Olympia: here 2,700 years ago the first Olympic Games took place ▶

TWO LEVELS OF EXISTENCE . . .

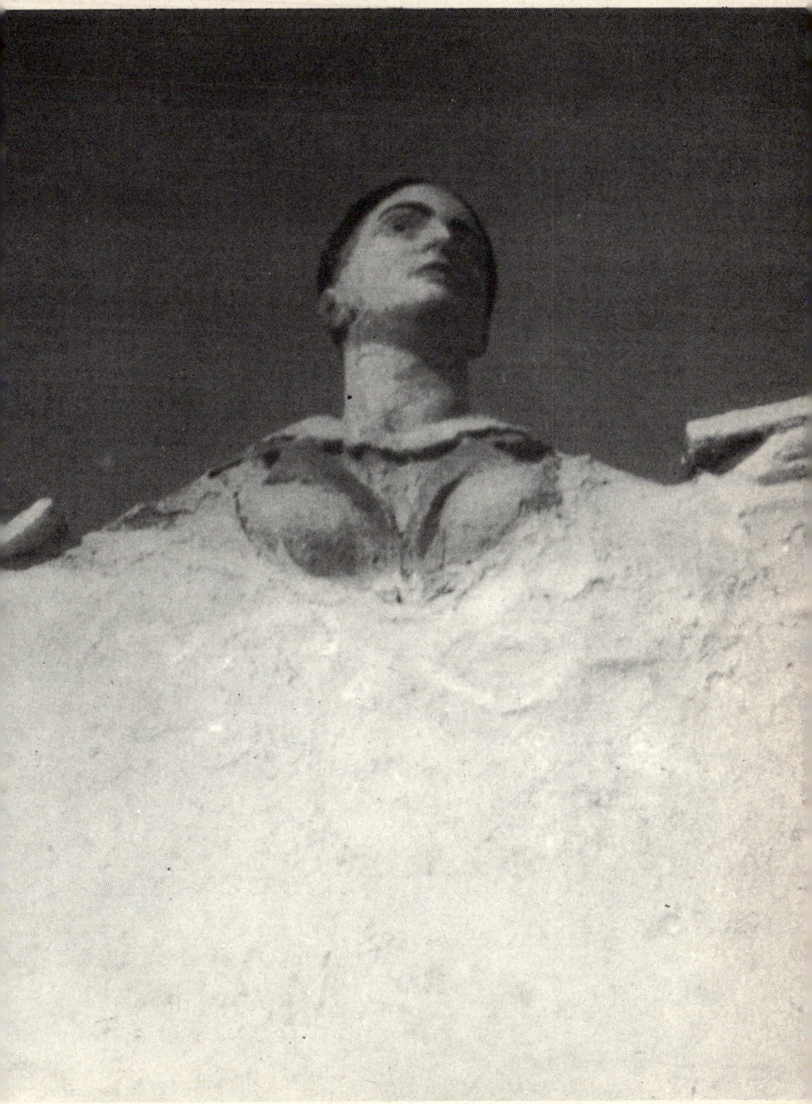

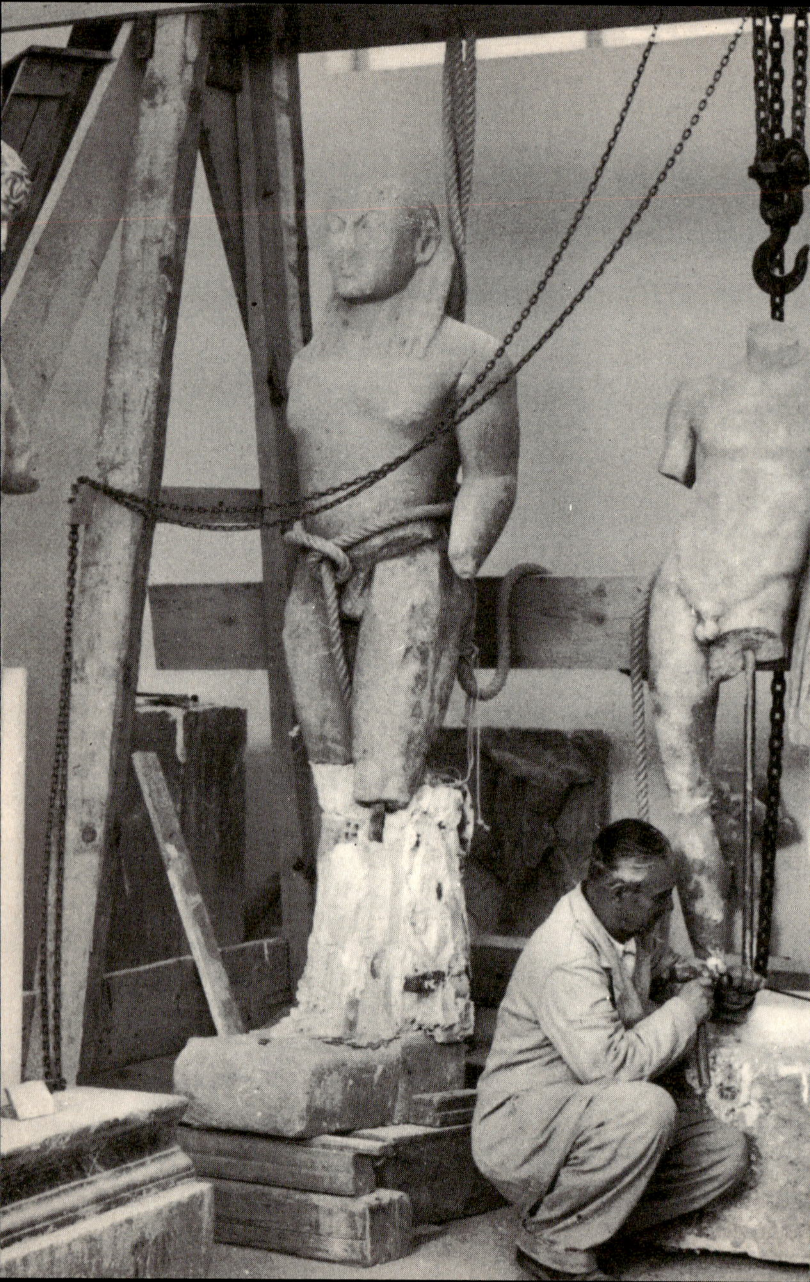

Parnassus

How lucky for a people to have no history to speak of; and luckier still not to have any ancestors, that is not to have "The Past" perpetually hanging over them like the Sword of Damocles.

History is a double-edged sword, as we have known ever since Freud. If you were a poet, philosopher, sculptor or dramatist, wouldn't you feel a bit uneasy about having had for ancestors Homer, Plato, Phidias or Aeschylus? Whether he accepts his ancient heritage or not, the modern Greek measures himself against it. This shouldn't be lost sight of when grappling with the cultural problems of modern Greece, dominated as they are by a perpetual quest for self-awareness. After all, what is more natural in a people cut off from its past by four centuries of slavery and then one fine day waking to find itself in the middle of modern times?

Yet those centuries were not entirely fruitless. The island of Crete in particular, before it fell into Turkish hands (1699), contributed two masterpieces of neo-Hellenic literature: *Abraham's Sacrifice* and *Erotocritos,* dramas in verse by Cornaros (17th century). It also enriched mankind with the paintings of El Greco (Domenicos Theotokopoulos). The noble figures of Rigas and Adamantios Corais are late 18th and 19th century forerunners of the "intellectual engagé", in the best sense of the word: they gave all their thought to the cause of national liberation and lent an attentive ear to the lessons of history. This was quite in accordance with the ideal of the ancient thinkers to whom reflection was a political act. Rigas moreover had to pay with his life for his "engagement". Austria, where he had taken refuge, handed him over to the Turks; who put him to death.

But it was not until after the Liberation that some organised form of literary and artistic life emerged. The War of Independence, whose turmoil lasted till 1830, gave the poets and writers plenty to write about. It inspired some of the great works of modern Greek literature. Such poems for example as the *Hymn to Liberty* (whose opening stanzas form the first lines of the Greek national anthem) and the *Besieged by Liberty* which was inspired by the fall of Missolonghi, both written by Dionysios Solomos (1798—1897). And in the realm of narrative prose, the *Military Memoirs* of Kassomoulis and the *Memoirs* of General Makriyannis, two racy chronicles of the long years of struggle, are also works of considerable literary merit. Makriyannis in particular, who was entirely self-educated, is one of the real literary geniuses of modern Greece.

After them, the deluge – that of the Romantics with all their paraphernalia of tears, sentimentality and precocious corpses. Yet they are contemporaries of Rimbaud. Finally, towards 1880, a generation blossomed which was to produce two of the greatest poets of the 20th century: Palamas and Cavafy. The first (1859—1943) is *the* national poet. Sonorous and eloquent, nay, torrential, talking at the top of his voice, he managed to give satisfactory utterance to that need of the heroic which is innate in every Greek. Cavafy on the other hand is much more modest and restrained; he lets silence speak. Living in Alexandria, he can keep aloof from those bizarre language quarrels and draws his vocabulary from all ages and all environments, without worrying about unity. He is practically untranslatable. So if you want to enjoy him to the full, you will have to learn Greek. Not that some translations of his work do not closely approximate to the spirit of the original; such as, for example, John Mavrogordato's rendering into English of a poem inspired by a remark of Plutarch about Mark Antony:

THE GOD ABANDONS ANTONY

When suddenly there is heard at midnight
A company passing invisible
With wonderful music, with voices, –
Your fortune giving way now, your works
Which have failed, the plans of a lifetime
All turned illusions, do not mourn uselessly.
As one prepared long since, courageously,
Say farewell to her, to Alexandria who is leaving.
Above all do not be tricked, never say it was
All a dream, and that your hearing was deceived;
Do not stoop to such vain hopes as these.
As one prepared long since, courageously,

As becomes one worthy as you were of such a city,
Firmly draw near the window,
And listen with emotion, but not
With the complainings and entreaties of cowards,
Listen, your last enjoyment, to the sounds,
The wonderful instruments of the mystic company,
And say farewell, farewell to Alexandria you are losing."

Like Proust, Cavafy did not and could not have any disciples, let alone found a school. Contemporary poets are of quite another species. Sikelianos is in the great lyric tradition, Seferis more akin to T. S. Eliot and Elytis to Eluard, whereas Engonopoulos remains faithful to surrealism.

The novel reached its full development in the 20th century with Papadiamandis, Xenopoulos, Myrivilis, Theotokas and Venezis. The case of Kazantzakis is a good illustration of the fate of Greek intellectuals. Since 1948 his books have been translated into English, French, German, Swedish, etc. And now at last they have been published in Greece. Why so belatedly? In the first place because publishers there are scarce; secondly because his books are thought to give offence, in particular his *Christ Re-crucified;* and finally because the author insisted on using the Cretan idiom – his native dialect – which annoyed the purists. Kazantzakis spent his last years in Antibes where he died in 1957; so the situation did not affect him directly. However it is more embarrassing for those who cannot or do not want to leave their country.

At first one might think that music and painting, being more universal languages than the language of words, would for that reason be free of the handicaps which face literature. That is not quite the case, though; at least not so far. Modern art batters against a resistance even from the intelligent section of the public. Abstract painting has not yet really penetrated Greece, neither has atonal music. (Nevertheless the country has presented the United States with a first rate conductor: Mitropoulos.) So the deeper reasons for what might be called this regionalism in literature and art must be sought, not in the realm of language, but elsewhere. Why is it that Greek artists and writers are so concerned to remain "authentic", while it would seldom occur to an English writer to think of himself first as English, and only afterwards as an artist? As to regionalism – one only has to remember works such as *The Power and the Glory, A Passage to India* and *The Good Earth* to realise how little this applies to English

[1] *The Poems of C. P. Cavafy.* Translated by John Mavrogordato. The Hogarth Press, London 1951, p. 26.

or American literature. Why then in Greece must every work of art at all cost "smell of thyme", to use a common expression?

The explanation probably lies in the country's recent past. In the four centuries of Turkish occupation the Greek got into the habit of establishing a strange relationship between himself and the foreigner. The foreigner, that meant the oppressor – therefore the enemy. The result of this identification of the foreigner with the enemy was a particular stress on all that was Greek; every national characteristic was regarded as a potential weapon and valued in terms of its capacity to resist the enemy. And one can't deny that historical developments in Greece, from the coming of Otto's Bavarians to that of the Americans in 1955, have given ample justification for the continuance of this state of mind. So it is only natural that the artist should feel really at home only in an environment which is, in a direct and immediate sense, his own. Only in contact with *his* soil, *his* sky, *his* light can he unfold his talents to the full. With the best contemporary painters such as Ghika, Tsarouchis, Moralis and Engonopoulos, this strong attachment to environment gives a special quality to their work, and has resulted in some fine pictures. But too often "picturesqueness" serves as an alibi and local colour takes the place of art.

It should be added that Greek folklore has an extraordinary power of expression. It has none of the lightness, *insouciance* of that of Naples or Nice. It is oriental, if you like; not, however, in its enchanting, colourful sense, but insofar as it has the same quality of horror, weightiness and gloom – even in its humour.

Take for example *Karaghiozi* (= Black Eyes, in Turkish), the popular hero of the galanty (shadow) show – a cross between Charlie Chaplin and Puck. Barefooted, with a huge, sensual nose jutting out over a black moustache, he is undoubtedly of Turkish, or rather oriental, origin; yet formed in the Greek mould. As in Chaplin films, hunger – the chronic hunger of the starving – is the theme of innumerable stories which have become almost proverbial. Looking through the window of a breadshop at the loaves piled in rows, Karaghiozi asks the baker in surprise: "*All that is yours, and you don't gobble it up?*" Karaghiozi dreams that he is sitting in a restaurant with a plate of noodles in front of him. "*Bring me some sauce*", he tells the waiter. The next moment, before the waiter returns, Karaghiozi wakes up. "*Idiot, you should have eaten them without sauce,*" he exclaims.

Karaghiozi is surrounded by Kollitiri (his son), Barba-Giorgo (his uncle), Hadjiavati (his friend) and a whole host of minor characters who together make up the cast of the galanty show. Spathari, a master in this form of art, has developed all these figures to perfection. Karaghiozi has even found his way – and with much success – into

the great arts, in particular the ballet, to whose choreography he has richly contributed.

The most moving expression of Greek folklore is the *rebetiko*. This is not so much a form of music as a documentary, a reportage. Are we not in the last resort "reporters", "witnesses" (which in Greek, you may remember, means the same as "martyrs"?).

What, precisely, is it? Not a popular song in the style of *Good King Wenceslas* or *Tannenbaum*. It is the complaint of a certain social group, that of the outcasts, the scum of the earth to put it bluntly. The song is usually accompanied by two or three string instruments, the famous *bouzoukia* – distant cousins of the mandolin and the balalaika. The rebetiko is primarily a dance, grave and full of allusions and double meanings. This is the *hassapiko* (= dance of the butchers) and consists of quiet, slow movements like those of a person sunk in meditation.

But one should not confuse this very special aspect of folklore with the conventional local colour which is more or less intended for export: evzones, peasant-dances and the like. That would be just as bad as confusing a West End or Broadway leg show with a Morris dance performance.

The Greek in general, and the Athenian in particular, is a gay spark. He loves festivities, weddings and meals in restaurants, which he likes to prolong till dawn. Throughout the year one feast-day follows another, and almost every day the calendar furnishes some excuse. For all the saints have someone or something to protect. St. Nicholas watches over the sailors; St. Barbara over the artillery; St. Demetrius over Salonika; St. Dionysius the Areopagite over Athens.

The most solemn feast of the year is Easter – the Greek Great Easter, the evening of Good Friday sparkling with stars and with wax candles . . . Through the city a large procession carries the dead God, shrouded in a cloak of violets and lilac. A beautiful death, whose slumber lasts only two days, long enough to prepare the Paschal lamb and the cakes. Thousands of little orange lights, the candles of the devout, pierce the darkness, and fireworks explode above the chanting of the popes (priests). No one stays indoors, not even unbelievers.

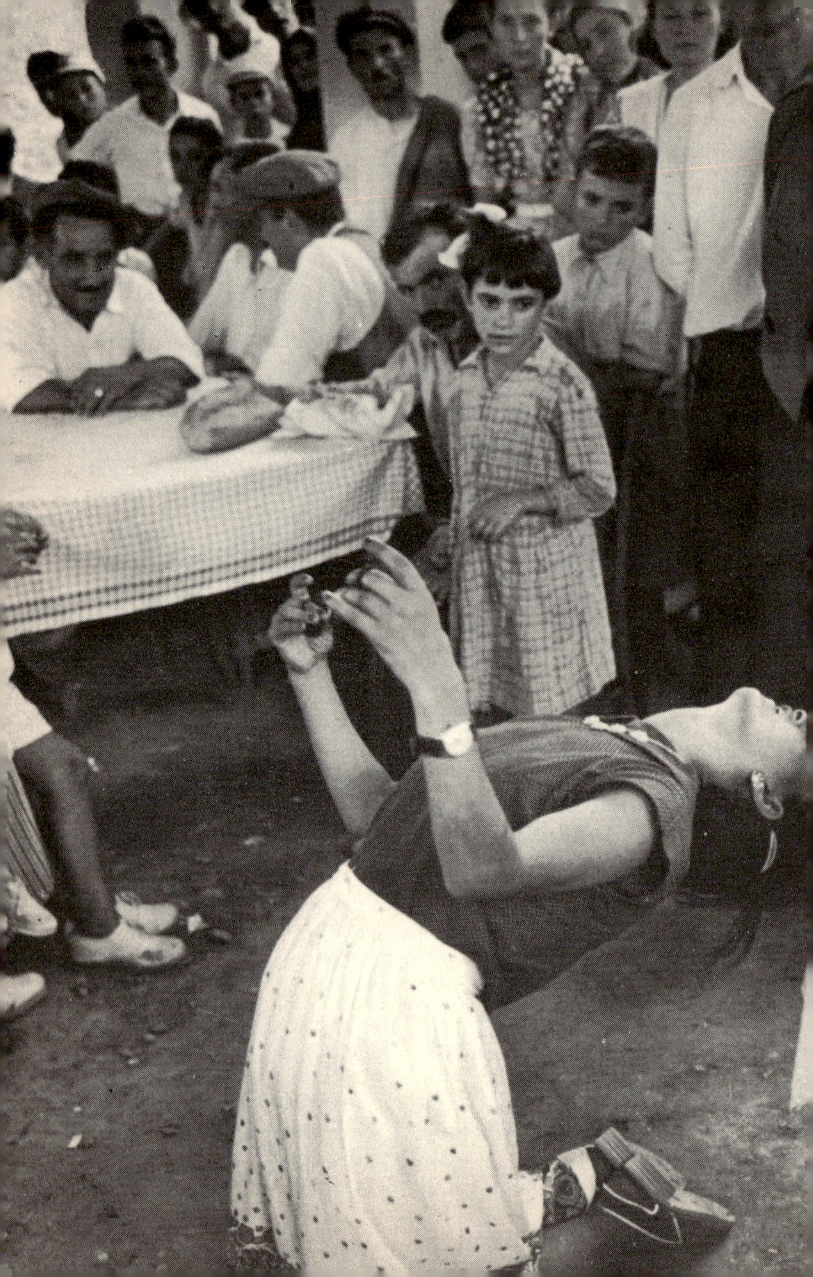

The Resurrection is celebrated at midnight on Saturday, usually in the open, in front of the churches. Spring is still in the air, with that slightly sharp tang of the first fine days. After mass, you go home to a meal of *maghiritsa* (= tripe soup) and Easter eggs. "*Christos anesti*" (Christ has risen), shouts your neighbour, knocking his egg against yours which you hold, as on a tripod, between three fingers. "*Alithos anesti*" (truly risen), you reply, cracking your egg in turn against his.

But the real feast of the Resurrection does not start until the great day itself. That is on Sunday morning, when the air is pure and full of the scent of lilacs. The Paschal lamb is roasted in the open on a spit flanked by *kokoretsi* (liver and kidneys skewered together and surrounded by miles of intestines coiled like paper streamers), and by *splinantero* (skewered milt). I'm speaking of the countryside, of course; in the towns these customs, along with so much else, are disappearing.

Around the spit the dance begins, to the accompaniment of a clarinet and a *santouri* (an instrument like a zither). It's the *kalamatianos,* a dance in the same style as the farandole of Provence, or else the *tsamikos,* the traditional dance of the heroic kleftes of 1821.

Beside their nests the newly-hatched crickets are busy. The year is starting anew; the wheat, green with hope, is springing up. The harvest promises to be good, and everybody has a pair of new boots to celebrate the Miracle of the Resurrection.

GREEK LITTLE

MALE EVZONE

FEMALE EVZONE

EVZONE

THEATRE 2 Modern Characters

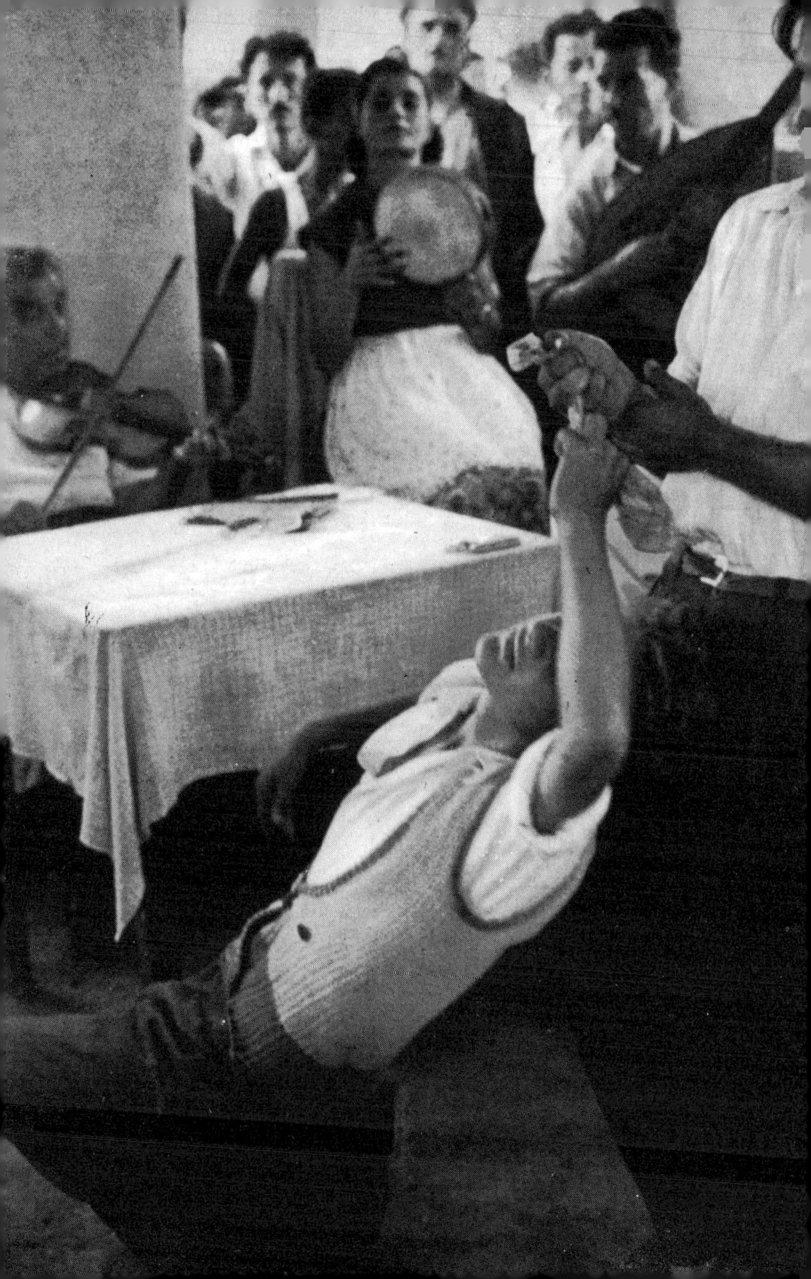

THE ODYSSEY

Athens and its surroundings

Athens is not an ugly capital, provided you don't, as in Andersen's fairy tale, mistake the beautiful little swan for an ugly duckling.

It spreads itself between the two hills of Lykabettos and the Acropolis, overflows them, submerges them, follows its course until the sea calls a halt. Thus it is almost linked with the Piraeus and Old Phaleron.

Its centre lies in between Constitution Square *(Syntagma)* and Concord Square *(Omonia)*. Between these two squares three roads run parallel – Stadium Street (since the Liberation called Winston Churchill Street), University Street (Avenue Venizelos) and Academy Street (Franklin Roosevelt Street).

University Street looks severe with its three neo-classical, Bavarian buildings dating from the eighteen thirties and forties: the National Library, the University, and the Academy. All this would be rather indifferent but for the saving grace of the white spire of the St. George chapel in the background, on the top of the Lykabettos.

Let's proceed by analogies – a quick if incorrect procedure. The Kolonaki quarter near the Royal Palace is a bit like Mayfair in London or the White House area in Washington. In the same way Hermes Street corresponds to Regent Street or Fifth Avenue. But there is no literary and artistic quarter in Athens like Chelsea or Greenwich Village. The literary and arty gentry gather between noon and two o'clock in the Loumidis café – no, I beg your pardon, the "Brazilian" – and stand about arguing for hours on end, pressed together as in the London Underground or the New York

◄ The University, or Genius spurring on Knowledge

subway at rush hour. Cheap and varied adventure lurks in the Omonia neighbourhood which in this respect has something of Soho or the streets running west from Times Square. Athens also has its "Field of Mars" – a bit greener than the Sahara, a bit yellower than an English park. It also has its miniature Hyde Park with lakes, swans, courting couples and all: the National Garden adjoining the Zappeion.

Like every self-respecting Greek, the Athenian spends a large part of his time in cafés. The Floca and the Zonars, near Constitution Square, are the smartest. They have ice-creams there, fantastic both in size and taste. The Zacharatos cafe, near the sumptuous St. George

Hotel, is the former meeting place of generals, admirals and other retired worthies.

To my knowledge nothing like the Plaka exists elsewhere. It is the old part of Athens, full of memories and dreams, which climbs hazardously up the rocky slope of the Acropolis. Its narrow little streets, leading to the summit through the smoke of the taverns, its secretive old houses and aroma of sweet-basil wipe out the commonplace impression of the modern town.

Nine times out of ten the traveller makes his first contact with Greece through Athens. Whether he has come by air to the airport of Elleniko (Hassan), or by sea to the Piraeus, or whether he has taken the easier Simplon route, he will unavoidably be landed here on

his day of arrival. Here he will have his first encounter with the Greeks.

They are short and solid, of medium height, smile rarely but chatter and gesticulate like mad. Do you think they look quite ordinary – a bit like Welshmen perhaps? You are wrong. For example, take a closer look at the evzones in front of the Monument of the Unknown Soldier (that's what they are there for, anyway: more or less for

Monument of the Unknown Soldier

show). Look at their stature, at the way their hips slope down. As symbols of courage and of love, and to be worthy of that gorgeous belt we know so well from the folk-dancers, they have to be well-built. And the women? Well . . . in general – mind you, in general – they are a bit more gross than French women, a bit harder than Italian women, but they are graver, more sturdy. I find it difficult to answer that delicate question you don't ask. Try, that's all I can say, and you will see. Even if they are not particularly forthcoming, who knows, you may be lucky . . . But virginity is closely guarded in these parts.

Come on! You are not here only for amusement. Better take Dionysius the Areopagite Street and improve yourself on the sacred hill of the Acropolis. The best way to approach the Acropolis is not through the Propylaea but through the Beule Gate (named after the French archaeologist who discovered it in 1853). Marble stairs – mind, they are slippery – lead to the Propylaea, the entrance to the

View of Athens from the Acropolis

Acropolis built by Pericles in 437, after the completion of the Parthenon. To the right of the Propylaea is the platform of the exquisite Ionian temple of Athena Nike or *Apteros Niki* (Wingless Victory), of Pentelikon marble. One might almost think that her wings were clipped deliberately, to prevent her from flying away from Attica.

For high up on this terrace the temptation is great: it is as though one would only have to leap into space to find oneself carried on air. Moreover, there have been precedents. Aegeus, Theseus' old father, stood on this same terrace looking out for his son's return. Theseus

The Acropolis

was on his way back from Crete, where he had just killed the Minotaur, and so giddy with his victory that he forgot to change the black sails of his ship, as he had promised. At the sight of those sails of mourning old Aegeus, thinking his son was lost, and crazed with grief, threw himself from the rock. I like to think his face was like that of King Lear.

But to turn to something more cheerful: look at the hills of Philopappos in front of you (Philopappos was a Roman prince of Syrian extraction who heaped benefactions on the Athenians; they were at that time badly in need of them and expressed their gratitude by erecting a monument over his tomb during the 2nd century A.D.). It's a favourite walk for courting couples: the ideal setting for love. With such a wonderfully clear view as far as Aegina it feels as if the whole world belonged to you – when there are two of you together on the southern slope of the Philopappos.

The grotto at the foot of the hill is called "Socrates' prison" – a label attached to it only by custom, for Socrates was never imprisoned here. Such customary names are very common in Greece. The Theseion for example, which you can see from the other side of the Acropolis, in front of the Agora, is not a temple of Theseus, but of Vulcan. Together with Demeter's temple at Paestum, this 5th century B.C. Doric temple is the best preserved in Greece. Why "Theseion"? Because of the sculptured frieze which does indeed depict the exploits of Theseus.

The theatre whose stage you can see at the foot of the Acropolis is the Odeon of Herodes Atticus. Its acoustics are perfect, and altogether it is quite an impressive affair, although it is Roman and dates only from 161 A.D. During the fine season it is often used for concerts and theatrical performances. The theatre of Dionysos, the foundations of which were laid in the 5th century B.C., can't be seen from here; it lies to the left of the Odeon. It seems strange that this lewd god – though perhaps appearances are deceptive – should be at the root of Tragedy. The primitive form of drama was the dithyramb, the sacred chant in honour of Dionysos. This theatre, though it has been reconstructed more than once, is thus one of the oldest theatres, since it goes back to the earliest times of classical tragedy.

But it's time to enter the Acropolis. Between the Propylaea and the Parthenon is an open space where something is missing. It's the spot where the colossal statue of Athena Promachos used to stand, Phidias' great creation. In the 6th century Justinian moved it to Constantinople.

On the very centre of the rock the Parthenon rises, like a vision of light. In common with all Greek temples it consists of a *pronaos* (entrance porch), a *sikos* (the temple proper) and an *opisthodome* (back porch). In the *sikos* used to stand the sumptuous ivory and gold statue of Athena Parthenos (the Virgin), also by Phidias.

The technical skill which gives the Parthenon, in contrast to the other, rather heavy, Doric temples, such an ethereal aspect calls to mind the egg of Christopher Columbus. Its base is not horizontal but slightly convex, and the vertical columns lean slightly inward. So every trace of stiffness is removed, and the building seems ready to fly away at any moment.

Beside the Parthenon, with ease and dignity the tireless Caryatides (more correctly *Korai)* support the weight of the Erechtheion (the

View of the Parthenon from the Propylaea

A PSALM IN COLUMNS

◄ Temple of Jupiter

Previous page: the Parthenon

temple of Erechtheus, a primitive Attic hero). They serve no purpose, for this Ionian temple doesn't look at all heavy. Conspicuous by its absence – though a cement casting takes its place – is the frieze removed to London by Lord Elgin . . . Next we set foot on the most ancient sanctuary of the city. On this very site the famous competition took place between Athena and Poseidon, with the city of Athens as its stake. Poseidon caused water to spurt from the ground: you can still see the well which his trident opened up. But Athena won: she raised up an olive tree. There it is, beside the Caryatides and immortal as they.

All Athenian life is centred around the Acropolis. Those noble cliffs to the right of the Beulé Gate, whose silence obliterates the noise of the town, are the Areopagus – the hill of Ares, god of war, once the seat of the criminal tribunal of Athens – and, further on, the Pnyx, where the people's assembly used to meet.

From there you can descend to the Agora, the American domain – I mean the domain of the American school of Archaeology. Recent finds have made possible the reconstruction of the Stoa of Attalus (2nd century B.C.) which nowadays rises up before our eyes in the full glory of its newness. (All foreign schools of archaeology in Greece have in some way their own territory: Delphi and Delos are the domain of the French, Crete used to be that of the British.) Here in the Agora the everyday life of the *polis* was carried on. The Athenians gathered under the porches – traces of which can still be seen – to acclaim or exile statesmen, or to listen to the philosophers. The most important buildings were the *Metroön* (official archives) and the *Bouleuterion* (= Senate). The round base to the right of the Theseion (looking towards the Agora) is the *Tholos*. It used to be the headquarters of the fifty Prytanes or magistrates who enjoyed free meals there at State expense. You will remember that Socrates, when his judges proposed that he should choose his own punishment, asked to be admitted to the Prytaneum.

Not far from the Agora the Ceramic Cemetery preserves a quality of silence which is different from that of living ruins: here the image of Athenian life is offset by the image of death.

If after hours of heroic and exhausting wandering in the Campidoglio Museum or the Vatican Museum, tired out by miles of masterpieces heaped in the room like potatoes after the harvest, you at last enter the Archaeological Museum of Athens (that of the Acropolis is closed), you sigh with relief and contentment: this is a *classical* museum in the fullest sense of the word; everything is in the right place – the exhibits, the pedestals, light, space, inscriptions. Every item has been treated with due respect. This perfect museum is the work of a couple who are both directors: Christos Carouzos and his wife.

It contains only a fraction of its pre-war riches. During the German occupation all ancient treasures had to be buried, for the fury of the enemy was directed indiscriminately against both the living and the dead – the immortals I should say.

In the first room you can follow the evolution of Greek ceramics. From severe and not very imaginative "geometric" vases (1000—700 B.C.) you pass on to more Oriental designs with a profusion of flora and fauna (700—600), then to Attic vases, first melanomorphic (i.e. black figures on a red background, 6th century), later on erythromorphic (red figures on a black background, 5th century).

Next, the distant, archaic smile of the Kouroi greets you, whilst further along the Zeus of Artemission (5th century) – a noble deity with a pointed beard, standing impatiently on his pedestal – busies himself with whatever he is doing. Or is it Poseidon perhaps, and does he hold in his hand not a thunderbolt, but a trident? The archaeologists can't make up their minds.

Before your eyes pass the most moving funeral steles of Attica. The beautiful Athenian woman who, with a very feminine smile, takes leave of her jewellery before descending into the underworld is called Higisso (daughter of) Proxenos. Her name is engraved at the bottom of the stele. Next you have a surprising encounter with someone you know quite well from Plato's *Symposium:* Diotima, who

inspired Socrates' doctrine on love and who also has her votive stele here. However if you prefer great art, you'd better fasten your eyes upon that bas-relief from Eleusis (5th century): Demeter, in the presence of Proserpina, hands an ear of corn to Triptolemos. These people, with their symbolic gestures and mysterious liturgy, are refugees here; you will meet them again in Eleusis, in their natural setting.

Finally, if you insist on getting a clearer conception of what precisely is the meaning of that vague term "neo-Hellenic" which in Greece is flung at you incessantly at every turn, you've got to visit the Benaki Museum. This is the private collection of Antoine Benakis. It is under the direction of another couple, the Hadjidaki, who are Byzantinists. (Not all Greek archaeology is carried on by couples, though!).

This museum harbours all sorts of things, e.g.: Greek costumes assembled from all over the country and very decorative; extremely fine jewellery which has nothing in common with the cheap junk sold in the shops; some very beautiful Byzantine and Cretan icons; two – not particularly good – El Grecos; magnificent embroideries, fabrics, innumerable articles of daily use (shepherd's crooks, distaffs etc.), an extraordinary collection of weapons and one of the engravings with which General Makriyannis' *Memoirs* were illustrated. The complete

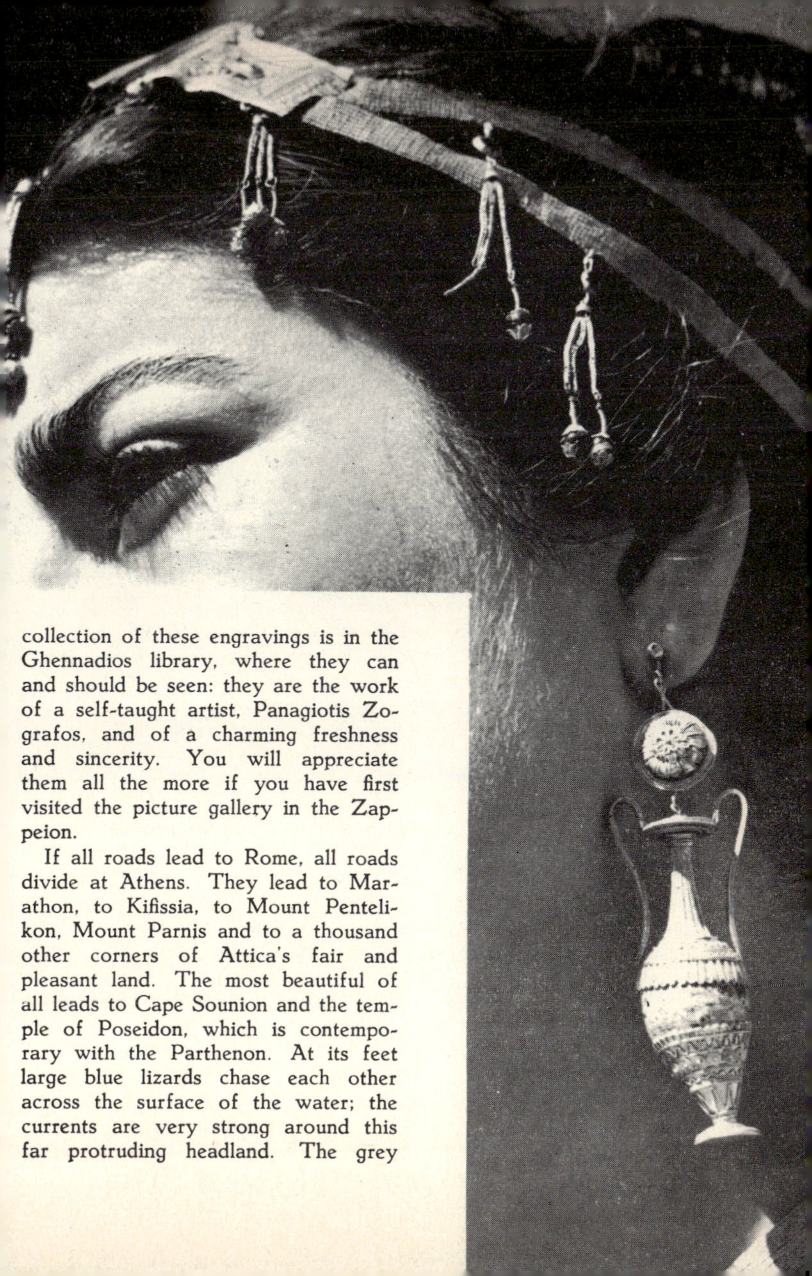

collection of these engravings is in the Ghennadios library, where they can and should be seen: they are the work of a self-taught artist, Panagiotis Zografos, and of a charming freshness and sincerity. You will appreciate them all the more if you have first visited the picture gallery in the Zappeion.

If all roads lead to Rome, all roads divide at Athens. They lead to Marathon, to Kifissia, to Mount Pentelikon, Mount Parnis and to a thousand other corners of Attica's fair and pleasant land. The most beautiful of all leads to Cape Sounion and the temple of Poseidon, which is contemporary with the Parthenon. At its feet large blue lizards chase each other across the surface of the water; the currents are very strong around this far protruding headland. The grey island which appears to be crouching on the sea, to the left of the temple, is Makronissos.

Is the landscape really as blue, as miraculous as it looks to me? Anyway, this is what I would like to be watching before I close my eyes for the last time.

On the road to Eleusis, a few miles from Athens, stands the small Byzantine church of Daphni. Daphni means "place of laurels". This

P. Zografos – Illustration for the *Memoirs* of General Makriyannis

pretty little spot is well known on account of the nearby mental hospital, and no less because of its 11th-century church, half hidden by cypresses.

The scenery here reminds one of Mozart at his best – it melts away in sweetness and pastel shades. In the cloisters, forgotten mornings of innocence and joy take on new life. Everything contributes to a cheerful, uncomplicated mood.

You enter the little cross-shaped church and look around. Presently you lift your head and there, without flashes of lightning or blaring of trumpets, the Day of Judgment is announced in the eyes of the

Pantocrator (Ruler of All Things) who glares down at you from underneath his terrifying eyebrows. This mosaic, in my opinion equalled only by the immense blue Madonna of Torcello, has been restored – though not very ably. But no matter, the Pantocrator – or, as Malraux puts it, Jupiter turned Pantocrator – retains his power to strike dismay into you.

Eleusis means "arrived". So it's time for us to leave; Demeter will see to the rest. The pilgrim of today follows the same sacred route which was described by Pausanias in a guide of the 2nd century. The Mysteries enacted Proserpina's abduction by Pluto, the god of the underworld, and Demeter's desperate search for her daughter. But over and above this symbolism they reflected the human tragedy itself, the drama of life and death. So they were celebrated at two different times of the year. The Minor Mysteries in the month of Anthestirion (more or less coinciding with March) celebrated Proserpina's ascent to earth, and the Great Mysteries a few months later, her descent to the underworld. A sacerdotal hierarchy led by the Hierophants formed the personnel of the Mysteries. The initiation proceeded in four successive stages, the first two of which were public. The procession of *mystes* (initiates) who went on foot to Eleusis started from the Eleusinion, Demeter's sanctuary which faces the Sacred Way. There was even some sort of communion, for the

mystes drank *Kykeon*, as Demeter did in her moments of greatest despair.

The initiates entered the Sanctuary of Eleusis through the same Great Propylaea which lead there today, and which precede the Little Propylaea. The large empty hall was the *telestirion* where the actual initiation took place. Of Demeter's Temple not much remains. Moreover, the chimneys of neighbouring soap factories somewhat spoil the scenery. Frankly, in Eleusis nowadays you have some difficulty in getting into the mood of the mystes.

However, there is still the way back, the Sacred Way of which one never tires. Once past Daphni, the descent to Athens is triumphal, and the view unique. It is one of those rare spots from which one can embrace the whole city from one end to the other – a city which retreats behind its lights.

There'll never be another day like this. But the one which awaits us tomorrow promises to be even more beautiful.

◂ Eleusis

The islands

"I do not know much about gods," as the poet said.[1] Like him, I think that the Archipelago is a white god broken to pieces – Zagreus or some other perhaps. Parts of his body are stranded on the coast of Asia Minor. They are the Dodecanese islands (Gothic Rhodes, Kalymnos – the island of sponge-fishers –, Kos, etc.). Another piece of the puzzle is anchored a little further off: Cyprus, most of whose inhabitants as everybody knows aspire simply to either re-union or independence. Other islands such as those in the Gulf of Saronikos, the Sporades (Skyros, Skiathos, Skopelos) and the Cyclades (Andros, Tinos, Paros, Naxos, Delos, Mykonos, Santorin or Tyra, etc.) sought protection near the mainland of Attica and Thessaly.

Next comes an agglomeration which halted midway between East and West. In many respects the Ionian islands form a kind of bridge between Italy and Greece. I won't say anything about Crete, for that is not a proper island: it is a sixth continent situated between Africa and Europe.

Finally there's a group of Naiads floating in the neighbourhood of the northern shores of Greece, I mean Thrace. They are called: Thassos, Chios, Mytilene, Samothrace.

Little boats bearing names like "Undine" or "Dolphin" ply daily between the Piraeus and the islands in the Gulf of Saronikos (Aegina, Poros, Hydra, Spetsai).

Aegina, at an hour's distance from the Piraeus and well sheltered from the winds which at times blow strongly across the Aegean sea, has a hothouse atmosphere. That's why those Aegean earthenware

[1] T. S. Eliot, *The Dry Salvages*. Faber & Faber 1941.

◀ Syros

jugs are like portable refrigerators and, during long summer journeys, keep the water fresh and cool. On this scorched soil rises the temple of Aphaia, an Aegean deity: it is as old as the Parthenon and just as beautiful, resting on the island as if in a casket made to measure.

A few hundred yards separate the adjoining island Poros from the Peloponnesian shore. Like giant plants in symmetrical vases pines sprout up on both sides. At a certain hour in the afternoon Poros reminds one of hai-kai: transparent porcelain; or simply of those shells called halyotis.

All the more striking is the contrast with nearby Hydra. Its bare cliffs, ending at the harbour entrance in cannon muzzles, bespeak courage, pride and glory. To the War of Independence Hydra contributed a fleet, numerous leaders and as many heroes. These sailors, grown wealthy in trade, lived in palaces of great charm and simplicity whose sly beauty and deceptive modesty bring to mind some of the finest abbeys in Europe. Like all houses in Greece, they are open to visitors. One of them (the Tambasis house) has been turned into a branch of the School of Arts. It offers accommodation to artists who come to work for a few weeks on this heroic soil, which leaves no room for complacency.

The round-trip by boat from Mykonos to Delos (or the voyage to Cythera) is a must. No journey to Greece is complete without a visit to Mykonos, which is very much the fashion – a bit like Capri. So far, it hasn't been spoilt by tourism. The inhabitants are as charming as ever, the prices as low, the amorous adventures as simple and gay. But I shudder to think that one day perhaps into these snow-white little streets, stained here and there with a red flower growing across a wall, public lavatories will spread; radios will be blaring through the silence of a moonlight night; and that no longer will a room with a sea-view be obtainable on this island on whose deserted beaches one can at present bathe naked.

But thank heavens it hasn't come to that yet, and Mykonos still retains that whiteness which defies all comparison with milk, chalk, dove or foam. It has three hundred and thirty-three churches; do you know why? For centuries Mykoniates have lived on piracy and salt water. And every time they suffered a setback they vowed to build a chapel if only the dear Lord or one of his saints would come to the rescue. Nowadays there is practically one chapel to every two houses.

From Mykonos the caique takes you to Delos in half an hour. The sacred island does not stand out as clearly as its name would make one believe (Delos = the obvious). Poseidon made it rise above the waves, apparently supporting it with diamond pillars. He created it to help Latona who was pregnant by Zeus and therefore relentlessly

Mykonos ▶

Delos – Terrace of the Lions

persecuted by Juno, that guardian angel of the conjugal hearth. So Latona was able to seek refuge on Delos and, on top of Mount Cyntha, give birth to Apollo and Artemis.

Both had their sanctuary on the sacred island where henceforth it was forbidden either to be born or to die. Thus Great Delos or Rhenea, the island opposite, served both as cemetery and maternity home. Every four years the Athenians organised the Delia festival, in honour of Apollo and Artemis, and sent a delegation – the *theoria* – on board two sacred vessels *(paralos, salaminia)*. During the festivities capital punishments were suspended in Athens; which is why Socrates had to wait for the return of the theoria before he could drink the hemlock.

In some ways Delos reminds one of Pompeii. Here, as there, the visitor walks through the streets of a living city with its houses, its shops, its temples, its brothels. In Pompeii, the houses are called *Casa dei Amorini Dorati, or dei Vetti.* In Delos it's House of Cleopatra, or House of the Trident, or House of the Dolphin. The architecture is the same, as essentially the Romans did no more than copy the Greek house. In Delos the mosaics are covered up, but at the price of a small tip it's easy to have them uncovered.

Another point of resemblance: the presence of alien cults and temples. In Pompeii, Roman baths co-exist with the temple of Isis. In Delos the two temples consecrated to Serapis, the Egyptian deity, are evidence of the existence of an important foreign colony. The whole Terrace of the Alien Gods, to the left of the Museum, is devoted to Syrian and Egyptian cults. But in Pompeii there is nothing like that archaic torso of Apollo (6th century) in his abandoned sanctuary, its very flesh still appearing to suffer from its mutilation; nor like the Terrace of the Lions, also archaic, yet how modern in conception, how near to us. Delos is the birthplace of the immortals. They are not intimidated by volcanos. On the contrary, Artemis and Apollo have subdued nature here and sometimes come to sit beside either the Sacred Port or the Trading Port, dreaming of that first dawn when Latona presented them with the splendid gift of life.

Next I would advise you to set sail for Crete, brown land of pirates and passions.

Until 1900 A.D. no one suspected what riches lay buried in the Cretan past. It is true to say that the excavations – and above all the finds – of Sir Arthur Evans at Knossos brought to light a new civilisation intermediate between those of Egypt and Greece. He, too, established the chronology of Crete:

— A first neolithic period ending before 3000 B.C.

— An ancient Minoan period – subdivided in three phases – running from 3000 to 2000. The vases of Kamares (the Cretan cave where

Delos – Torso of archaic Apollo

they were discovered), which can be admired in the museum at Heraklion date from this period.

— A middle Minoan period (2000—1700 B.C.), subdivided in I, II and III is the great age of Crete during which the first palaces of Knossos and Phaestos were built.

— Finally, the late Minoan period (I, II, III, till 1400) which witnessed a second - and last - Renaissance. On the ruins of the first palaces of Knossos and Phaestos new ones arose, the same whose ruins can still be seen today. After that, no more was heard of Crete. The Mycenaean civilisation put in an appearance, and the centre of gravity moved to the Greek mainland.

Crete is nowadays one of the most prosperous regions of Greece. Oil, raisins and oranges of excellent quality ensure the Cretans (whose names usually end with *-akis*, as those of Spartans do with *-akos)* a certain measure of comfort. This enables them to enjoy the good things of life. Big, brown, brawny and rowdy, above their black boots they wear the *vraka*, trousers wrinkled in the same way as those of odalisks. They love dancing, especially the whirling *pentozali* which no one but they manage to do properly. They are also fond of singing, above all *mantinades:* lyrical, mordant, smutty stanzas at the end repeated in chorus.

Do you remember Tassoula? The beautiful Cretan whose abduction nearly unleashed another Trojan war in 1951? Well, don't worry. Our present-day Trojan wars end quite simply in the divorce-court. The violent and passionate aspect of the Cretan temperament does not show on the surface, at least not in Heraklion or Candia, the capital of Crete. Like Eleusis, it is disappointingly dismal and commonplace. But there is always the Museum - one of the most beautiful it has ever been my fortune to see. The Louvre, the British Museum, Italy's museums are all chock-full of Greek art. But Cretan art can only be seen here, on the soil where it originated and where the lover of modern art - in other words pre-Hellenic art - will feel at home. Moreover the museum is under the direction of an archeologist of exceptional knowledge and refinement, Mr Plato.

The ornaments, precious stones, implements, vases - all have something exotic that is only found again, though less pronouncedly, in Mycenaean objects. Look for example at this collection of *rhyta* (a kind of drinking vessel). Have you ever seen anything quite so graceful as this one with the bull's head? You can hardly tear yourself away from it.

As you wander from room to room, watchful eyes are following you: those of the octopuses and other sea creatures which decorate the Cretan vases, so much more fantastic, variegated and daring than their Attic counterparts.

Very prominently displayed is the enigmatic, undecipherable disc of Phaestos which holds the secret of Cretan writing. You will get even with it yet: he laughs best who laughs last.

The sense of walking in an archaic paradise grows stronger in the room adorned with the frescoes of the Cretan palaces. It is upholstered in seraphic blue and Corrida red – a red so appropriate to Crete, combining the colour of its dry earth with that of blood. The famous Prince of the Lilies is coming towards you, arrayed in his dignity and his loin-cloth. The "Parisienne", pardon me, "Minoenne" with her high bosom, pinched waist and mischievous smile seems to think the story she keeps to herself very funny. She often reminds me, goodness knows why, of the Etruscan Apollo in the Villa Julia in Rome – the Apollo of Veii.

The palace of Knossos on the hill of Heraklion was partly reconstructed by Sir Arthur Evans in a praiseworthy attempt at popularisation. The few landmarks he set up indeed enable one to get some idea of the lay-out of the bullfight-stained palace where King Minos dwelt. It was built round about 1800 B.C. to take the place of another that had been destroyed, and it was in fact the famous Labyrinth. The construction of this complicated, exitless building has been ascribed to Daedalus. The legend correctly based itself on the assumption that a tree is known by its fruit and that, when one's name is Daedalus (= cunningly wrought), one cannot but build labyrinths. Whence this word? It comes from *labrys*, which means double axe – a symbol which is found all over the palace of Knossos and was the emblem of the Minotaur, the god of Crete, and of the priests of the religion dedicated to him.

Minos, the legendary master of this palace, was the son of Zeus and Europa, which partly explains his twofold character of man and beast; for Zeus took on the guise of a bull to seduce and abduct Europa. After nine years' apprenticeship with his father, Minos went to Crete and became the venerated king and legislator of this island. His great wisdom earned him the esteem of the immortals, who extended his post of arbitrator and censor into the hereafter: they made him one of the three judges *(Kritai)* in Hades, along with Aeacus and Rhadamanthus.

In one respect Minos was at fault, and posterity, in particular Attica, had to pay dearly for this: his marriage with Pasiphae. This lady, whose tastes were a bit peculiar, deceived her husband with a bull and in due course gave birth to the Minotaur, half man half bull. When Minos found out, he fell into a truly Cretan rage. He shut the animal up in the Labyrinth where it stayed for years, satiating itself with human blood until Theseus put an end to it.

At this point another, more humane, legend takes over: that of

The Prince of the Lilies ▶

Theseus and Ariadne which still echoes in the basements of the Labyrinth. Minos made the people of Attica pay a heavy tribute; once every nine years they had to send to Crete seven youths and seven maidens, chosen from the most noble families to be fed to the Minotaur. Theseus took it upon himself to free his country from this burden. He entered the Labyrinth, killed the Minotaur and managed to find his way out again thanks to the guiding thread provided by Ariadne, the daughter of King Minos.

Is this a symbol of love defying all obstacles and labyrinths? Or does it signify the supercession of Cretan civilisation by Aegean

civilisation? Anyway, the hasty traveller will find all this rather bloodthirsty and Spanish. It will probably remind him of Mexico, of the Aztecs, the Grand-Guignol or Boris Karloff. But he is wrong. For on the southern slope of Crete is the white palace of Phaestos. As

in Knossos, there are really two. A first palace, built around 2000 B.C., and a second – the one you are looking at – which was destroyed about 1400 B.C. If the epithet "royal" means anything at all, it applies here. The palace, which is built in tiers, dominates the plain, the sea, yes even time. In the tourist pavilion Alexander, the immutable keeper, also defies the ages. (Certain people in Greece seem

Cretan vase

to be destined for immortality during their lifetime, to such an extent have they become identified with the life of the country: Captain Loizos for example, the boatman of Mykonos, or Vassilainas, the Rabelaisian restaurant keeper at the Piraeus).

And that little fishing village a few miles from here seems to have found the right word, the word one was looking for: it is called Aghia-Galini, Saint Serenity.

Postscript to Crete: the tour Heraklion—Rethymo—Canea. Canea has given a great statesman to Greece: Eleutherios Venizelos. He rests up there, on the Belvedere which bears the name of Akrotiri (the Cape). On his marble tomb an epitaph composed by himself is engraved. The noise and tumult of a long life full of struggle has at last died away. Only the murmur of the pine-trees now protects the slumber of the just. For mile upon mile the beaches stretch into the distance. There is no end to the sixth continent.

Cretan ►

Appendix to the islands:

SANTORIN OR TYRA

CORFU

SYPHNOS

AEGINA

HYDRA

Water every day

POROS

Fruit every night

TINOS ▶

A miracle every year

The Peloponnesian tour

Up to 1882 the Peloponnesus, that mulberry leaf (which in modern Greek is actually called *Morias* [Morea], was linked to the Greek mainland by a thin umbilical cord. In that year on the isthmus of Corinth a French company began a project which, finished in 1893 by a Greek concern, cut a canal across the isthmus. Thus the Peloponnesus became a proper island, the island of Pelops, son of Tantalus. Let's say at once that Pelops was of Lydian origin, which partly explains the utterly oriental cruelty of his fate. His loving and thirsty papa Tantalus served him up to the gods during a banquet, by way of a main dish. It was for his own good, though: being digested by the gods meant becoming part of the divine essence. But the gods wouldn't hear of it and restored Pelops to his father. From then onward his name was bound up with Peloponnesian history. We will meet him again at Olympia.

The olives of Kalamai, the raisins of Corinth, the fruits and vegetables of Argos have nowadays made the Peloponnesus an area of primary importance economically. The "Morean", i.e. Peloponnesian, is intelligent, even crafty; he is also obstinate, conservative and, in general, has "arrived". He treats "Roumeliots" with a certain amount of condescension; for the inhabitants of Roumelia, that part of the Greek mainland which stretches southward from Thessaly to the Gulf of Corinth, are courageous but rather limited, and sometimes even dumb. The "Morean" is also resentful. In the region of Mani (around Sparta), the Greek equivalent of the French Vendée, the Vendetta is still honoured.

From the time of the Metaxas dictatorship to the present, the most

◀ Mistra

competent members of the Security Corps have been recruited in this region.

The road connecting Athens with Corinth is in every respect one of the most beautiful roads in Greece. Beyond the canal, as far as the eye can see, stretch the blond tips of the vines. The fact that the Corinthian raisin has no pips is a Godsend – one of two miracles in Greece. The other is a boneless fish, the "Calamare" which can be prepared in thirty-six different ways.

A few miles further on, at Xylokastro, is a holiday-camp – one of the biggest in Greece after the one that the Mediterranean Club runs on Corfu. It attracts not only foreign campers, but also a whole host of natives of the stronger sex. These overheated Southerners are much impressed with the exotic beauty of the foreign girls; but marriage is another thing altogether. On this subject a Greek proverb counsels: *"A home-made shoe, even if it is patched, is preferable."*

Here begins the verdant and prosperous plain of Argolis, Greece's kitchen garden. Apart from tragedy, Argos produces melting and fragrant melons which, together with water-melons and large glasses of water, are the indispensable accessories of a Greek summer.

Normally, the traveller will pass the first night of his Peloponnesian journey in Nauplia. He won't regret it; in the first place because Nauplia, the first capital of modern Greece, is very picturesque. That pretty little island at the entrance of the Gulf seems to have come straight out of a Japanese print. It is called Burzi and in the olden days used to be the home of the executioner. But we make progress; nowadays the executioners live amongst us. And thus Burzi has been turned into a comfortable hotel, just a tiny bit "thrilling" because of its past. The two eagles' nests which dominate Nauplia are the fortresses of Akronauplia and Palamedes; they are reached by a stair of 999 steps (I haven't counted them). You will observe there is no "bridge of sighs". So the prisoners could groan as much as they liked, no one would hear them. Their voices, like their lives, were walled in, following the ancient tradition of Antigone. Fortunately these prisons are no longer in use.

No doubt all this strikes the enchanted traveller as pretty barbaric. But he will spend a night free from fleas, and rise fresh and fit next morning for the famous drive to Epidaurus, to see the Theatre, the Sanctuary of Aesculapius, the walls of Tiryns and, finally, to be off to Mycenae.

There he is face to face with the natural setting of tragedy. In Mycenae the sky is eternally grey, even if the sun has chased the last fringes of cloud from the rest of Greece. Perhaps the walls breathe sadness; or memories; or unsatiated hatred which oceans of blood have not been able to extinguish. The Atrides inherited their thirst for blood from their ancestor Tantalus. Their history is that of Cain and Abel poured into the mould of Greek tragedy.

Atreus and Thyestes, sons of Pelops and grandsons of Tantalus, had taken refuge with Sthenelos, king of Mycenae. When the latter died, the inhabitants of Mycenae decided to elect as their king one of Pelops' sons. Thyestes suggested they should chose the one who could produce a golden fleece. He had his reasons for this. Atreus accepted the proposal. He also had his reasons; for some time before

Mycenae

he had discovered amongst his herds a lamb with a golden fleece. He kept his secret carefully and had no idea that his wife, who was Thyestes' mistress, had had the fleece sheared and given it to her lover. At the appropriate moment, Thyestes alone could produce the fleece and was elected king.

However, man proposes, god disposes. On this day of treachery, a miracle occurred: the sun set in the East, and the Mycenaeans concluded that the gods disapproved the choice of Thyestes. So Atreus took power and started his reign by killing the three sons of Thyestes and serving them to their father to eat during a banquet. Afterwards he showed their heads to Thyestes, revealed the contents of the dish and banned him from the town.

Thyestes had another son: Aegisthos. Atreus had two: Agamemnon and Menelaus. So the tragedy continued. Agamemnon married Clytemnestra and led the Achaeans to the Trojan war. When he returned, his cousin Aegisthos had usurped his place. Possession is nine points of the law; so on the advice of his mistress Aegisthos killed Agamemnon. This crime brought the couple a few years of peace, until Orestes, Agamemnon's son, revenged his father by eliminating them both.

The epilogue to this slaughter is to be found in the museum of Naples. It is the statue of Orestes and Electra, orphaned by crime and sick of it all. It always reminds me of the day after a great shipwreck, when a board floats on the water bearing the name of the ship: *The Intrepid*.

The tomb of Agamemnon – the so-called "treasure of Atreus" – and that of Clytemnestra are some distance away, to be out of harm's way most likely. But in spite of this precaution they may not be interred there at all: the archeologists are not sure, for the royal burial place used to be inside the Mycenaean Acropolis, to the right of the Gate of Lions (and what Lions!). It was here that Schliemann, a self-educated archaeologist of genius, decided to start his excavations. He discovered treasures in the real sense of the word (jewellery, implements and various other objects) which justified Sophocles' description in the *Electra:* "Mycenae rich in gold" *(polychrisis)*.

A comfortable, nay royal road leads from the burial ground to the palace, as if to show how simple and direct was the connection between these two . . . Not all the psychoanalysis of our age can make this palace of madness and horror any the less sinister. The death-like appearance of the grey plateau has a chilling effect, and the sharp peaks below seem to be waiting to receive you in case you should be overcome by dizziness. Nothing is lacking in this doomed spot, not even an element of farce: the palace is surmounted by a temple.

Mistra, two and a half miles from Sparta, is less instructive but more soothing than Mycenae; one breathes more freely here. Goethe thought so, too, for of all places he chose this as the setting for Faust's meeting with Helen, in the second part of *Faust*. In true classical style he wrote:

"So many years deserted stood the valley-hills that in the rear of Sparta northwards rise aloft, behind Taygetus; whence, as yet a

nimble brook, Eurotas downward rolls, and then, along our vale by reed-beds broadly flowing, nourishes your swans." [1]

The medieval town of Mistra dates from 1249, i.e. from the days when Guillaume de Villehardouin took it into his head to build a fortress there with the purpose of fortifying the principality of Achaia. That was the name given to the Peloponnesus when it was a Frankish province; for in those days, you should remember, the whole of Greece was occupied by the Franks . . . A few years later, Mistra was reconquered by the Byzantines (1262); then came the Turkish occupation (1460).

Strangely enough, the administrative and political decline from the 13th to the 15th century was accompanied by a simultaneous flowering of Byzantine painting and architecture. This paradoxical situation is explained by the desire of the local lords, as they strengthened their power, to emphasize their independence in every possible way; for example by erecting churches and other buildings, to display their wealth and generosity. The little church of St. Sophia in Mistra was built by the "Despot" Kantakouzinos (from 1348 to 1460 Mistra was the capital of the Morea, the Byzantine name for the province of the Peloponnesus). The church of Pantanassa (1428), one of the most beautiful churches of Mistra, owes its existence to Janos Frangopoulos, prime minister of the Morea. In the same way the Perivleptos was built by laymen, whose names have been forgotten by now.

The Biblical figures in the frescoes have nothing in common with the art of Ravenna or of St. Sophia. Rather they illustrate Malraux's remark about Byzantium: *"Those centuries which were discovering the sublimity of tears were not to show a single weeping face, and this New Testament which was shaking the world to its foundations left no other traces of its passage, on the walls, than the august faces of the Old Testament worthies. What was once called man at Salamis was yet again becoming a mere fleeting shadow."*

At the end of the Peloponnesian trip, along the shores of the Alphios, the laurels of Olympia wait to crown that modern athlete: the tourist. In his honour Pindar's ghost whispers new songs from the shades of Mount Kronion: the odes of this poet are all dedicated to victors in the ancient Games – those of Olympia, Nemea, Isthmos and Delphi.

We also owe to Pindar our first information about the origin of the Olympic Games. They come from the funereal games which took place near Pelops' tomb. From 776 B.C. onward they were celebrated

[1] Johann Wolfgang von Goethe, *Faust* Second Part Act III. Translated by Bayard Taylor. Ward Lock, and Co., London and New York, 1890.

Reconstruction of Olympia

regularly every four years, until the Christian zeal of the Emperor Theodosius II finally suppressed them (393 A.D.).

Olympia was not a city properly speaking, but a sacred enclosure. The Altis – the sacred olive wood – supplied the *kotinos*, the precious branch which crowned the heads of the victors. The Games were presided over first by one, then two, and finally by several judges who acted as referees between the Hellenes flocking there from all parts of Greece. During the festival, which in Pindar's days (5th century B.C.) lasted a week, the *spondophores* (sacred heralds) travelled all over the country to announce the *ekechiria*, the suspension of hostilities. Access to the Stadium was barred to married women, but not to girls.

Before taking part in the Games, the athletes took the oath before the statue of Zeus Horkios (Zeus of the Oaths). They swore to abstain from using any unfair practices to gain victory. The programme of contests included running (sprint, long distance, and in heavy armour); discus and javelin throwing; wrestling; boxing; chariot and horse races. Those beautiful athletic bodies, which by no means lacked spirit either, also competed at Marathon and Salamis. They served as inspiration for the sculptors and realised the most beautiful ideal of those times: perfect harmony between body and mind.

Probably in the hope of recapturing this ancient harmony, Baron Pierre de Coubertin undertook to revive the Olympics in 1896. His heart lies buried in Olympia, in the midst of the old stones he tried to restore to life.

In this city of sportsmen race-tracks take up the largest area. That of Palestra was reserved for wrestling contests. The Gymnasium was the training ground for runners; the Hippodrome was for horse-racing. Olympia was a sacred place; that is why it is full of those same "treasuries", little votive chapels, which lie along the Sacred Way at Delphi. The Heraion, a Doric temple dedicated to Juno or Hera (7th century B.C.), is one of the best preserved buildings.

But the temple of Zeus (5th century) was Olympia's greatest glory. In its *cella,* where the Greeks always used to put the statue of the deity in whose honour the temple had been built, stood Phidias'

Temple of Zeus

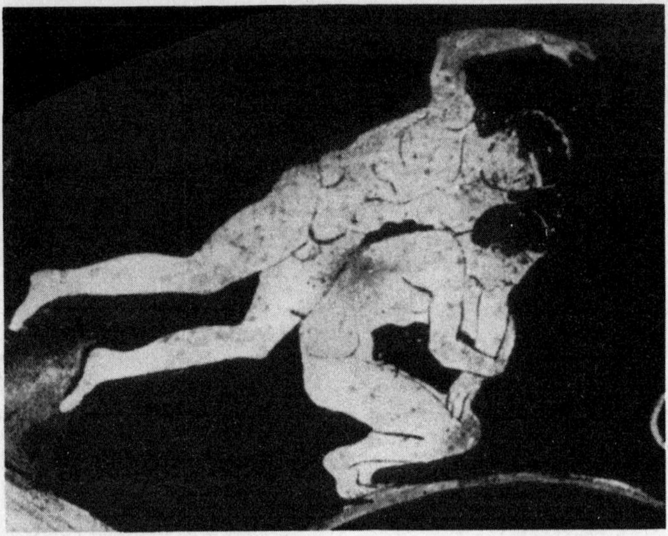

statue of the Olympian Zeus. It was mounted on a pedestal over two yards high and, like the Athena of the Parthenon, was made of ivory and gold – sumptuous materials which the Athenians used only for the greatest occasions. Phidias' workshop is nearby, and it is here that the masterpiece was conceived and executed.

In the museum of Olympia you can get a vague idea of what this temple must have been like. Two sides of the museum's main room are taken up by the sculptures of the two pediments. On the right are those of the western pediment, depicting the "Struggle between Centaurs and Lapithae" at the wedding of Pirithoös – a struggle in which, of course, the "eternal feminine" was at stake. The theme of the pediment on the left-hand side is the contest between Pelops and Oenomaos. Pindar is with us once more, for he related this story, which somehow has a medieval touch. Oenomaos used to subject all the suitors of his daughter Hippodamia to a difficult test: they had to compete with himself in a chariot race. He was sure to win, for he could count on the speed of two invincible horses. According to the terms of the contest, victory entitled him to put his vanquished adversary to death. Several young men had in this way departed this life for the hereafter.

However, Pelops went about it differently. He bribed the keeper

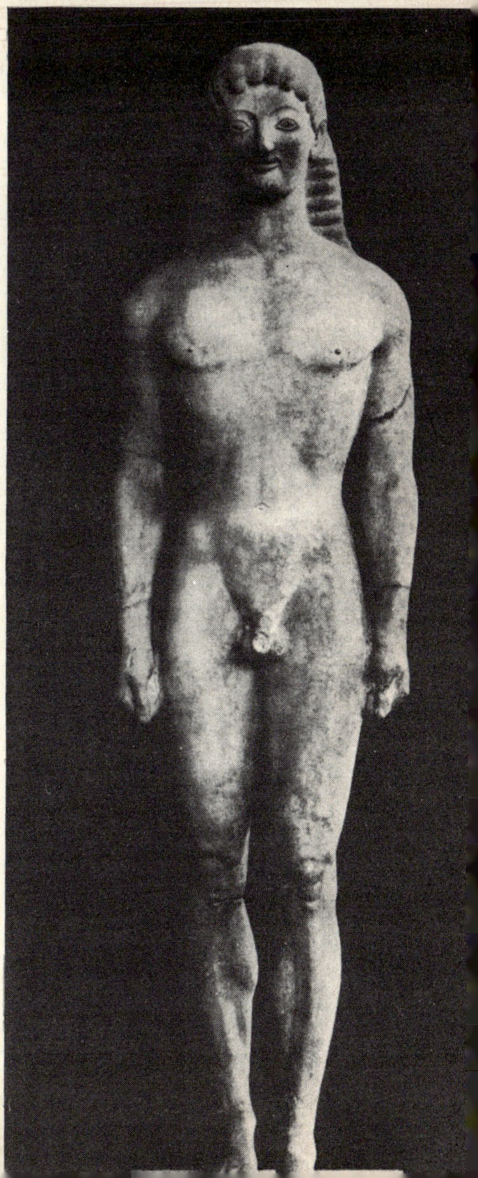

The Apollo of Tenea

of Œnomaos' stable, with the result that the latter, in the middle of the race, lost one of the wheels of his chariot. Everybody took it for granted that this piece of sabotage was an accident, and Pelops obtained the hand of Hippodamia – and therewith the Peloponnesus.

The same museum contains two other famous pieces of ancient sculpture: the Victory of Paionios (5th century B.C.) and the Hermes of Praxiteles (4th century). Swathed in her veils, the Victory looks more feminine than her counterpart of Samothrace; she is less of an Archangel as she advances towards us with a spontaneous movement. The Hermes of Praxiteles scorns all praise. Not that he repulses you – but he is entirely self-sufficient and rests within the perfect arc formed by his own suppleness and unity. And from the height of this spherical perfection he looks down on you with the ghost of a condescending smile.

Of all the aspects of antiquity, the Olympic spirit has remained most vividly and actually alive. The present-day sportsman feels closer to the athlete of antiquity than, for example, the modern artist to Phidias. Thus the human body, that most fragile of all elements, has best resisted the onslaught of time and has managed to remain the same. There is a paradox here, though perhaps not an obvious one. For man has been created with a mature body and an immature soul; so his body has to have intelligence and power enough for two, otherwise it would risk being smashed to pieces under the tremendous impact of the human adventure. It has to be stronger than the soul in order to be able to support the latter's weaknesses and gently to put it back onto its own road, namely that of immortality. Is not that the message of Olympia to an epoch which has lost its sense of harmony?

Cape Sounion, the southern tip of Attica
Ruins of the Temple of Poseidon

ΕΛΠΑ
ΔΙΣΤΟΜΟΝ-ΟΣΙΟΝ ΛΟΥΚΑΝ
DHISTOMON-OSIOS LOUKAS
VEEDOL
ΠΡΟΣ ΔΕΛΦΟΥΣ
TO DELPHI

Delphi

Our twentieth-century Odysseus has a sense of scenery; he has also a sense of fervour, though he won't admit it. So the last two days of his Odyssey are devoted to Delphi.

Off he goes once more on the road from Daphni to Eleusis, either by car or by coach, for there is no direct train to Delphi. Beyond Eleusis the road forks and he takes the left turning, whence it starts zigzagging up to the summit of the Kithairon – a beautiful road lined with pine trees and with wonderful views all the way. After two hours Odysseus, satiated with panoramas, at last reaches Thebes, a Boeotian town if ever there was one. He stops just long enough to gobble a spoonful of white mastic (thyme) jam – in the local jargon called a "submarine" – and to drink a glass of water; and then the plain of Livadia, covered with flowering cotton, stretches before him. On his way through he waves to the Lion of Chaeronaea without, however, managing to cheer it up: not all those centuries have been able to efface its leonine gravity and the painful memory of the Macedonian victory over the Greeks.

Presently Odysseus has the somewhat uneasy feeling of flying in an aeroplane: as it gains height the car, struggling with curves and precipices, appears to leave the ground and to float on air. With clenched fists and constricted throat he watches the yawning gorges grow wider and deeper. But his nausea soon passes and undamaged he is landed at Arachova, a noble old town on the outskirts of Delphi, where most beautiful woollen carpets are woven by hand. One more bend in the road, and there is Delphi, with the Kastalia Fountain and

◀ On the way to Delphi
The cross-roads where Oedipus killed his father

the Phaidriades rocks spread around in a semi-circle.

So many heights and so much roaring of subterranean waters; so many eagles and so many premonitions – this spot could never be a simple dwelling-place for humans. Thus it was first consecrated to the chthonian (terrestial) gods: to Gè (Earth) Themis and to Poseidon, to earth and water. Perched on her tripod, the Pythia chewed laurel leaves and made her prophecies near the cave where the serpent Python lived. Only later did this place acquire the name of Delphi – derived from Apollo Delphinios (the Dolphin), an island god whose cult had been adopted by the inhabitants of Krissa, the harbour of Delphi. This substitution of the Apollonian religion for the chthonian was, as all historical events in Greece, symbolised in a legend: the myth of Apollo who had to kill the serpent Python (dragon?) in order to take its place.

From the 7th century B.C. onward Delphi became the centre of the amphiktions, partly political, partly religious associations formed by a number of adjacent states who wanted to establish friendly relations between themselves (*amphiktions* = neighbours). These confederations were always centred on a temple. The most famous of these amphiktions was the one which gathered every spring in Delphi, and every autumn at Thermopylae.

But Delphi was most renowned for its oracle, which played such a big part in the political life of Greece. It is curious that these oracles are hardly ever mentioned by Homer who, when it comes to auguries, usually speaks of dreams and omens interpreted by soothsayers. Later, however, oracles became more frequent, and that of Delphi soon gained special prestige. This prestige in turn led to an accumulation of riches; for each question put to the oracle was accompanied by a compulsory offering, the size of which was not without influence on the Pythia and the personnel of the sanctuary. The silence of the oracle could truly be called golden. It was notorious that the Pythia "collaborated" after her own fashion; having "persianised" before Salamis – i.e. favoured the Persians –, she "laconised" during the Peloponnesian war and "philippized" – i.e. encouraged Philip – when the Macedonians invaded Greece.

Yet this did not detract at all from the oracle's reputation, for this was founded above all on the ambiguity of the replies. *"If you cross the river Halys, you will destroy a mighty empire,"*[1] was the Pythia's reply to Croesus, king of Lydia. Thinking that this applied to his enemy, Persia, he crossed the river. But it was his own kingdom which was destroyed.

[1] Herodotus, *The Histories.* Translated by Aubrey de Selincourt. Book One, p. 32. Penguin Classics.

Porch of the Athenians ►

Everywhere in Delphi, under the olive trees and amidst the scents of mint and thyme, one senses something sacred, hallowed. No doubt this is illusory, but what does it matter: you are overcome by a feeling of joy, of elation and you want to caress those old stones with their knowing look.

The sanctuary of Athena Pronaia (in front of the Temple) or Pronoia (Providence) was to a certain extent the ante-chamber of the sanctuary of Apollo, of the *temenos*. Two temples dating from different periods were consecrated to the goddess. You reach them by a path which starts under the plane-trees of the Kastalia Fountain. Between these temples are the ruins of the Tholos, a 5th-century, ring-like construction in marble, and one of the best preserved buildings of Delphi. In the adjoining gymnasium the athletes who were to take part in the Pythian Games in the stadium used to exercise. You will meet them again up there.

For this whole group of buildings is after all nothing but the entrance to the sanctuary of Apollo. The Sacred Way leading there starts higher up, to the right of the Kastalia Fountain. As Plutarch remarked in his little work on the "Oracles of the Pythia", it is lined with monuments and temples celebrating victories of Greeks over Greeks, such as that of the Phocians over the Thessalians, of the *Amphiktions* over the Phocians, etc. One exception, reminding one of a starry hour of the ancient world, is the "treasury" of the Athenians, built in honour of Miltiades out of the booty of Marathon. These "treasuries" one meets so frequently in Greece were chapels for receiving offerings to the gods presented on the occasion of this or that event.

The temple of Apollo rises above victories and human passions. Here we find ourselves at the heart of the world, a heart which pulsated in the subterranean part (the *adyton)* of the temple, where the *omphalos* (navel) lay hidden: a stone symbolising the exact centre of the world.

The theatre a little higher up (4th century B.C.) does not belong to the ruins proper. In the first place because it has been exceedingly well preserved. But also because it is still in use. It frequently rings with the cries of Oedipus, Orestes or Prometheus in modern Greek, and Terpsichore's feet once more touch the ancient soil of its *orchestra*. The Stadium, finally, surmounts the sanctuary. There the Pythian Games were celebrated, at first once every eight years, later every four, in memory of Apollo's victory over the Python. It may not be the centre of the world, but it certainly stands on a privileged spot, from which you can embrace the whole universe in all its transparency.

It takes quite a bit of resolution to tear oneself away and descend

◀ Temple of Apollo

to the museum. Such strength of character deserves a reward, which is offered in the person of the Auriga (charioteer) sitting in his chariot as taut as a dart. Don't be taken in by his serious demeanour, for he is not to be trusted. Often this mischievous child gives you the slip and stations himself at the entrance to the Archaeological Museum in Athens.

The sacred and the profane are closely allied. In this same neighbourhood occurred the tragedy of Oedipus. At a crossroads not far from Delphi he killed his father Laios before marrying, in Thebes, his mother Jocasta. And on this same place of incest and parricide Oedipus performed the solemn feat which has made him, together with Prometheus, the hero of the human species: he managed to solve the riddle of the Sphinx, thus liberating Thebes from this monster. Henceforward the answer was known; the animal which gets up in the morning on four feet, becomes two-legged at noon and threelegged towards evening is – man.

"The Inner Being (Essence)," says Hegel in this context, *"of Nature is Thought, which has its existence only in the human consciousness. But that time-honoured antique solution given by Oedipus – who thus shows himself possessed of knowledge – is connected with a dire ignorance of the character of his own actions."* [1]

Indeed Oedipus has no inkling he is giving the history of mankind and Tragedy its first impetus; that the queen of Thebes he is going to marry is his mother; that his daughter Antigone is going to pay for her father's deeds by in turn defending man against the animal, and her brother's life against Creon's orders. Oedipus could not foresee that thirty centuries later on these same mountains, people sitting in this same theatre would read their own destiny in his blood-covered face from which, driven by guilt, he had himself torn out the eyes. Nor could he have dreamt that they would recognize their own voice in his terrible complaint: " To which corner of the world can I take my sufferings? Where can I crush my voice? Oh qod, where have you led me!"

Your last day in Greece has come – a day of regrets and of memories. As to regrets, I remind you of the story of the bottle: an optimist and a pessimist are looking at the same bottle. "It is half empty", says the latter. "Oh no, it is half full", replies the first.

Half empty, since you have missed out the extraordinary experience of Mount Athos, which by itself would require a week, and the island of Rhodes with its palaces and wonders, and the Ionian Islands some

[1] Georg Wilhelm Friedrich Hegel, *The Philosophy of History.* Translated by J. Sibree, M.A. Willey Brook Co. New York, 1944.

The Sphinx ▶

of which escaped the earthquake of 1953, and the monasteries of Meteora in Thessaly, perched on those Ku-klux-klan-like cliffs, and Macedonia, and Epirus, and . . ., and . . .

But nevertheless the bottle is half full at the same time, and there you are, suddenly looking desperately for souvenirs.

First there are those friends you are not particularly fond of. The shops in Stadium street, with their trinkets, scarves made in Athens with the Parthenon printed on, and the like will cater for them.

But what about the ones you are fond of? For them you'd better go a bit farther afield and take a look at the antique shops in Pandros street. With all due respect, it is somewhat like the Via Babuino in Rome or London's Bermondsey market. With luck, knowledge, patience and, above all, some money to spend you will be able to pick

Meteora

◄ Mount Athos

up a beautiful antique vase with a pedigree, or a little statuette, or something else . . .

And then there is nothing more but to await the hour of departure in one of those cafés which already seem so far away. Goodbye to the monumental ices and the large glasses of water, to the rose-petal jam, pistachio nuts, orange blossom and aubergines (eggplants). Those chairs don't seem to be willing to let go of you.

Then the plane leaves the ground, the ship has snapped its ropes, the soil of the gods is slipping out of sight. One after the other the islands say goodnight before going to sleep, half-formed sentences still on their lips. Already the light is distant.

For you, the traveller who is about to be reclaimed by others, Cavafy wrote these lines: *"Poor though you find it, Ithaca has not cheated you. Wise as you have become, with all your experience, you will have understood the meaning of an Ithaca."* [1]

And do not forget, stranger, to tell Sparta that we are still here, three hundred of us, though many fell by the way, intent on deuphering its laws. The key to the mystery still escapes us, but we are seeking, we burn with desire. When shall we find it?

[1] *The Poems of C. P. Cavafy,* p. 48.

Four ages of Greece

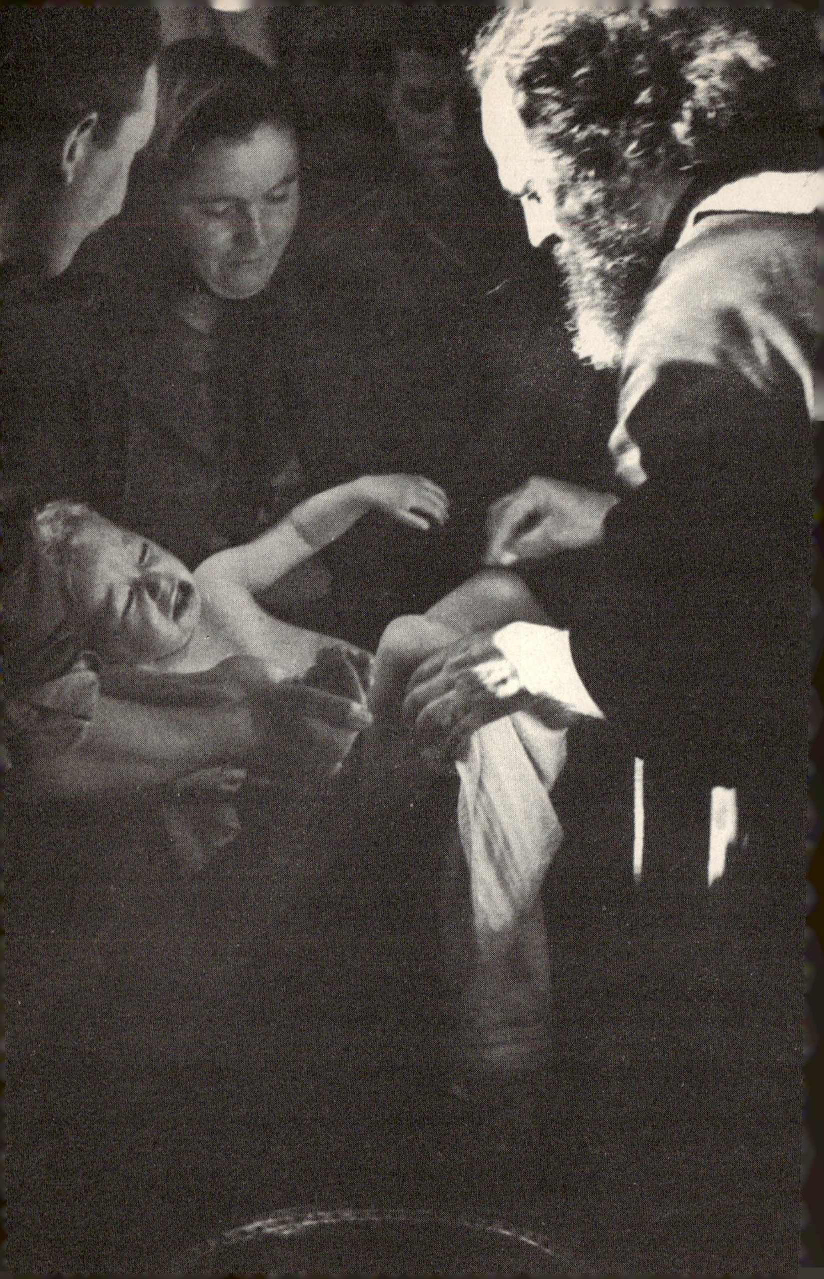

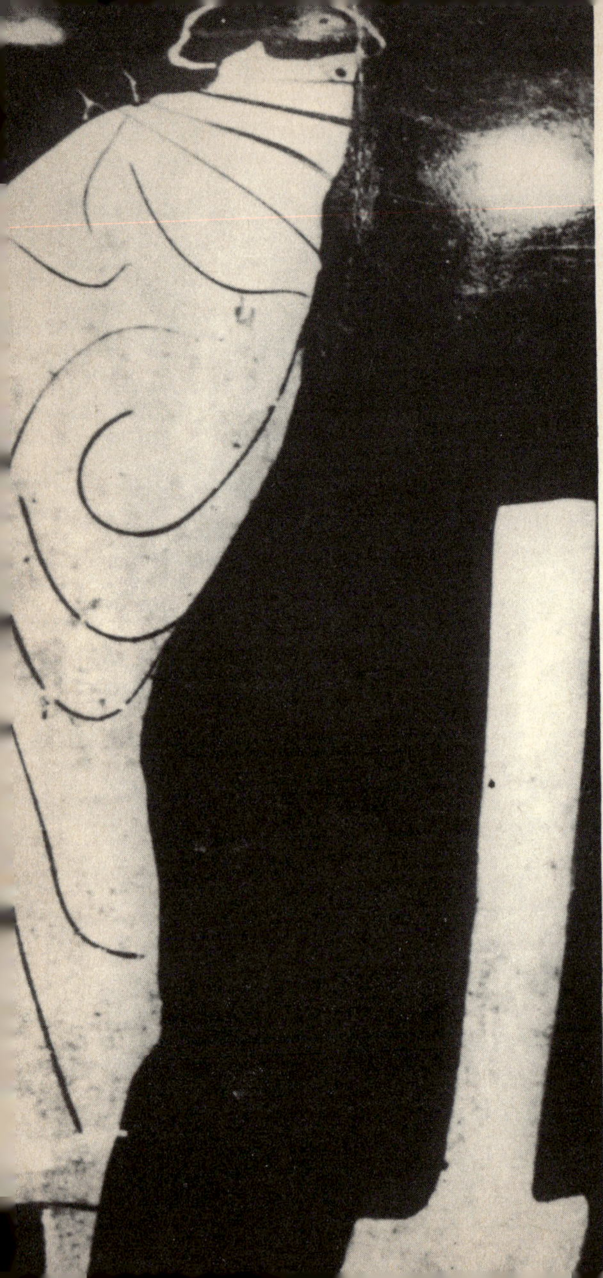

FOR

A TRAVELLER

"It needs a lot of obstinacy on the part of the foreigner and a lot of goodwill on the part of the restaurant owner before a typically Greek meal appears on the table," so someone wrote recently in his Memoirs. His chapter on Greece, food section, ends on the following beautiful note: *"Greek culinary talents, if not entirely non-existent, are to say the least very limited."*

Don't you believe it, traveller. You won't have to be obstinate at all to get served with Greek dishes. All you have to do is to ask for them anywhere, even in such a sophisticated "European" outfit as the *Averof* in Stadium Street. The only difficulty is one of choice.

The *mezedis* (hors d'œuvre) often takes the place of a full meal. Most typical varieties are: *avgotaracho* (mullet roes), *taramosalata* a kind of mayonnaise with fish roes, cucumbers, aubergines or pimentos in vinegar which go by the global name of *toursia* and, above all, *kokoretsi:* skewered liver, milt and onions tied together with entrails.

Entrées: an enormous variety of pies *(pita)*, cheese, chicken, vegetables. A particular entrée which is rather heavy and indigestible but delicious all the same is *moussaka.*

Main dishes: lamb or sucking pig roasted on the spit; stuffed vine-leaves with all the etceteras: aubergines, pimentos, tomatoes, cabbage leaves, marrow and even spleen.

Fish: Heading the bill, but rather expensive, is the red mullet – fried, grilled, pickled, smelling of the open seas and caught, so one says, in nets of silk. You will unavoidably have to try *marida,* a fried

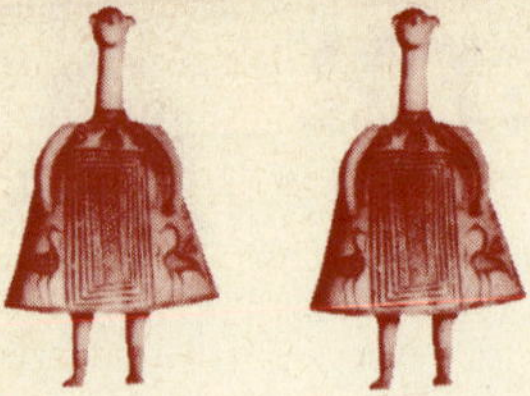

fish mixture basted in retsina, the celebrated resinated wine particularly common in Athens. It is a staple dish in taverns, as are *calamares* and octopus prepared in a thousand and one different ways: with vinegar, tomato sauce, baked in the oven, wrapped in paper, etc.; but it grieves me to think that nine times out of ten you will not have a chance to taste *petalia*, a fish quartered and dried in the sun and eaten almost raw – a speciality of the fishermen of Missolonghi.

Salad of wild dandelions or of mashed aubergines sprinkled with marjoram usually accompanies a fish or meat dish. But basil is not used, as elsewhere, to season tomato salads; as a vestige of olden times it blossoms in flowerpots and, from the window-sills, protects innocent idylls and serenades of lovers.

The *fèta* or the *manouri* of Crete are extremely noble cheeses. As to resin wine, it usually takes a little while to get accustomed to it. How long precisely depends on whether or not you like tart drinks with a taste of burnt wood. Don't get used to it too much; for this delicate golden beverage does not stand up very well to transport; it is difficult to obtain abroad and very expensive – quite unlike such popular dessert wines as Samos, Mavrodaphni, etc.

Preserves, a speciality of the island of Chios, are exquisite and very varied: morello cherry, bitter orange, citrus flower, rose petal – these are not the names of geishas, but simply a few out of innumerable different flavours. In general, Greek pastry is excellent. And if you like your sweets high-powered, you're bound to fall for *baklava, cadaif* and *courabies*.

One of the attractions of Greece is the almost total absence of amenities for tourists. And so, taking up your quarters with the inhabitants, you won't feel you are depriving yourself of palaces or sumptuous bathrooms. But Greece has discovered the tourist, and hotels are rapidly being built.

The natural response of the Greek, especially the peasant, is hospitable. You are not his guest, you are one of the family. The mistress of the house will produce from her trunk a pair of sheets – often the only pair – which she once embroidered with her own hands. In the morning she will bring you a cup of Turkish coffee a little bigger than a thimble, honey, brown bread and all she can scrape together in the way of butter in this land of stones and goats. If you admire the enormous conch on the chimney piece she will make you a present of it and force you to accept it. If you are not too keen on the smell of cooking in oil, her insistence may put you off a little, the more so as it is sometimes accompanied by a whole list of questions as to your social and financial status, your profession, etc. Never mind, take it with a dose of humour, disentangle yourself and remember that your landlady at home knows a lot more about you without ever having asked a thing. And anyway, Kyra-Leni or whatever her name may be does not criticize you; she won't make any the less effort to please you. She still lives in a pre-capitalist era and has pretty vague notions about the functions of money. She wouldn't denounce you to the police for anything in the world; on the contrary, if you were in any difficulty she would do anything to help.

Another tricky problem: what is the traveller to do with his evenings? In the country he can watch the darkness and be watched in return; or he can accompany the fishermen on their fantastic fishing expeditions by lamplight *(Pyrophani)*. In the towns he must proceed by dichotomy (division by two). First hypothesis: the traveller is dizzy with fatigue and sleep. Second possibility: he thinks that there'll always be time enough to sleep when he returns home. In the latter case he has the choice between: 1) The open-air cinema, a wonderful southern invention which allows one to sip an iced drink while finding out which films to avoid. 2) Open-air concerts in the theatre of Herodes Atticus. The setting will make him dream of a thousand unlikely things, of eternity, genius and music. 3) Three nights per month, at full moon and the nights before and after, the Parthenon stays open till midnight (the rest of the time it closes at 5 p.m.). Don't miss this opportunity; you will carry away a very clear picture of unreality and also some notions about space, the Mediterranean, and memory. 4) In the same theatre of Herodes Atticus, and sometimes in that of Delphi or Epidaurus, you can go and see one of the ancient tragedies (the Oresteia, Prometheus, Hecuba or Hippolytus) played in modern Greek. Until further notice this is the best thing the Greek theatre has to offer. If you have some vague school-days' memories you are bound to understand the text. People who knew no English could follow Laurence Olivier's rendering of King Lear. 5) Finally, for moonless evenings, there are the *bouzoukia*, which divide the neo-Hellenes into two opposing camps: fans, and the rest. The latter will explain that the craze for this musical drug is nothing but snobbism and that the "sensible" part of the Greek population will not have anything to do with it, contenting

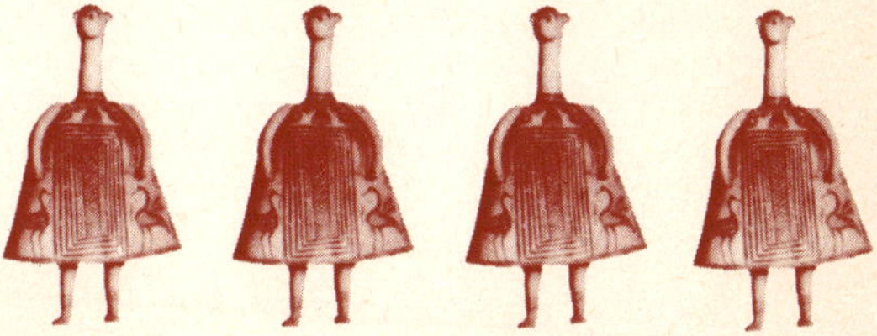

themselves with Italian canzonettas. The former will equally fervently want to initiate you into the secrets of this mysterious god and to show you the privileged places where he appears in his purest form. Of course you are all for authenticity, for the non-sophisticated article. But why, after all? In *Helzapoppin*, doesn't the true Russian prince who disguises himself as a fake one in order to be more convincing, give you food for thought? There is no need, for the sake of your love for *bouzoukia*, to venture out into distant suburbs with impossible names. Just take the bus and get off at Aï-Sosti, Singros Boulevard, or at Triana. The *bouzoukias* there are genuine, the linen more or less clean, the food very good and the prices reasonable. 6) There are also open-air dance places, which should be avoided by all but surtax-payers. They bear exotic names like "Miami", "Argentina" and "Chez Lapin", thus holding promise of whisky and even fruit juice.

One last piece of advice: if you want to save time, take the plane to Crete, Rhodes or anywhere else. That way you also gain a bird's-eye view of the Archipelago.

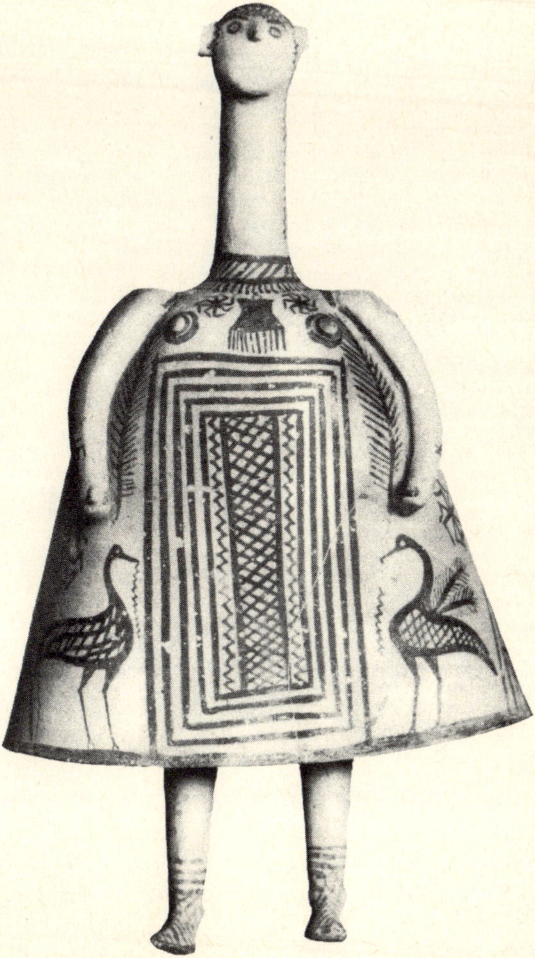

words . . .

English is fairly widely understood in Greece, so you shouldn't have too much difficulty in making contact with people. If you learnt Greek at school, this might be a help provided you pronounce it like everybody else – i.e. like the person you are talking to. There are for instance several ways of spelling the ee-sound:

ει (e.g. τρεῖς = three)	are all pronounced ee.
οι (e.g. πλοῖο = boat)	
η (e.g. μητέρα = mother)	
υ (e.g. νύχτα = night)	
ι (e.g. πριν = before)	

αι (e.g. ναι = yes) is pronounced as in maid.

ϑ (e.g. Αϑήνα = Athens) is pronounced as the th in "thought".

δ (e.g. δέντρο = tree) is pronounced as the th in "there".

γ (e.g. γάμος = marriage) is pronounced as the y in Yarmouth.

χ (e.g. χαρά = joy) is pronounced h as in Harvard.

ζ (e.g. ζωή = life) is pronounced z as in zoo.

αυ is pronounced as the case may be, either as af or as av. The same is true for ευ (ef or ev).

behaviour . . .

Except in very select places, you call a waiter by clapping your hands. To say "no" you shake your head, lift your eyebrows and make a little noise like "tts." Five fingers spread out like a rising sun in front of somebody else's face is an insulting gesture, expressing deep contempt *(mountza, faskelo)*. According to the Greek Orthodox custom, the sign of the cross is made by the three middle fingers held together and moving them first down, then right to left.

travel necessities . . .

politeness

Greeks are not given to shaking hands. However you can use the familiar form of address, i.e. in Greek the second person singular, to practically everybody: waiters, taxi-drivers, shopkeepers. "Yassou" is a greeting which can mean, according to the circumstances, good day, good evening, good night, so long, goodbye, etc.

numbers

Write them down (in the usual Arab numerals), that's the simplest way.

inquiries

πόσο (posso) = how much
πότε (paut) = when
ποῦ (pou) = where

times

αὔριο (avrio) = tomorrow
χτές (ktès) = yesterday
σήμερα (seemera) = today
Κυριακή (kyriaki) = Sunday
παντα (panda) = always
ποτέ (potè) = never

space

μακρυὰ (makria) = far
κοντὰ (konta) = near
ἐδῶ (edo) = here
δρόμος (dromos) = way, road

meals

νερὸ (nero) = water
κρασί (krassi) = wine
ψωμι (psomi) = bread
ψὰρι (psari) = fish
φροῦτα (frouta) = fruit
ἀγόρι (agori) = boy, waiter
κορίτσι (koritsi) = girl, waitress
ἔλα μαζί μου (ela mazi mou) = come with me

movement . . .

φεύγω (fevgo) = to depart
ἔρχομαι (erchomai) = to arrive
κολύμπι (kolybi) = swimming
ψὰρεμα (psarema) = fishing

. . . and its opposite

ὕπνος (hypnos) = sleep
σπίτι (spiti) = house
ξενοδοχεῖο (xenodochio) = hotel
δωμὰτιο (thomatio) = room

the untranslatable . . .

Κεφι (Kefi) means spirit, liveliness, animation, go; carried to the extreme by the prefix tsakir- (kèfi).
μερακι (meraki) means the enthusiastic care that is bestowed on living creatures as well as on objects and activities such as interior decoration or the preparation of a dish.

The greatest compliment one can pay anybody is summed up in the epithet *levendis*. It implies nobility, generosity and a certain measure of youth.

. . . and its opposite

There are many words of Latin origin (train, passport, valise, etc.) which have been taken over by modern Greek practically without alteration.

figures . . .

Population — 8,357,526 (census of March 19th, 1961).

Area — mainland: 41,328 sq. miles: islands: 9,854. Total cultivated about 3,400,000 acres or 5,312 sq. miles.

Production (in metric tons) -

	1960	1961
Wheat	1,692,023	1,593,837
Tomatoes	454,500	549,877
Olive oil and olives	80,494	312,074
Cotton	184,000	277,000

Trade (1961) — Exports: $ 234,300,000; imports: $ 561,200,000.

Exports (in thousand U.S. dollars) -

	1960	1961
Currants, raisins, fresh fruit	37,935	44,945
Tobacco	72,399	80,711
Cotton	19,183	27,398

Imports —

	1960	1961
Foodstuffs	93,605	100,041
Machinery	78,140	99,715
Petrol products	43,719	43,546

Tourists — 254,250 tourists visited Greece in 1958, and 440,243 in 1961.

weights and measures . . .

Meausures of length: the picque (or 64 centimetres) subdivided into eighths (roupta).

Weights: the ocque (1,280 grammes or 400 dramia).

Money: the drachm. The official rate of exchange at present is as follows:

1 pound sterling	84 drachms
1 dollar	30 ,,

These values were established in the spectacular currency reform of 1954 which made 1 new drachm the equivalent of 1000 old drachms. In spite of this the measure failed to strengthen the drachm's purchasing power. Generally speaking, life in Greece is a good deal cheaper than in Britain or the United States.

facts . . .

Visas are not required for British and American passports. Various categories of travellers (students, etc.) are allowed considerable reductions on return tickets. Information available at travel agencies.

Shops are open from 8.30 a.m. to 1 p.m. and from 3.30 p.m. to 7 p.m. in winter; from 8 a.m. to 1 p.m. and from 5 p.m. to 8 p.m. in summer.

addresses . . .

Athens:

British Embassy, 4 Odos Gennadiou.
United States Embassy, Mavili Square.
Bank of Greece, Panepistimiou Street.
Britisch School of Archaeology, Odos Souedias.
American School of Archaeology, Odos Souedias.
B.E.A. (British European Airways), 2 Amalias Street, & Othonos Street.
Olympic Airways, 6, Othonos Street.
Thos. Cook & Son, Ltd., 6 Philhellenes Street.
American Express Co. Inc., 2, Sintagma Square.
National Tourist Organization, Stadiou Street, Panepistimiou Street & Omonia Square.
E.L.P.A. (Greek Touring and Automobile Club), Panepistimiou Street.
Central Post Office, Kotzia Square.
Anglican Religious Services: St Paul's Church, Philhellenes Street.
Roman Catholic Services: St Denis, Panepistimiou Street.

Some restaurants and bars:

Platanos, 4, Diogenous Street.
Gerofinikas, 10, Pindarou Street.
Xynou, 4, Angelou Geronda Street.
Vassilainas, Piraeus, 4 Aetolikou Street.
Apotsos (ouzo and Mezedes), 5 Stadiou Street.
Pantheon, 73, Panepistimiou Street.
Averof, corner of Nikis and Mitropoleos Streets.
Kostis, 2, Korai Street.

Souvenirs:

Antique shops, junk shops, copper-smiths, etc. can be found in plenty in and around Ermou Street at the far end from Sintagma Square. There are many shops specializing in Greek popular art in the streets near Sintagma Square.

London:

Greek Embassy, 51, Upper Brook Street, W.1.
Greek State Tourist Office, 195 Regent Street, W.1.

Washington:

Royal Greek Embassy Information Office, 2211 Massachusetts Ave., N.W. 8.
American Express Co. Inc., 622 14th St., N.W. 5.

New York:

Greek Consulate General, RCA Building, 1250 Avenue of Americas.
Royal Greek Embassy Information Office, 120 East 56th St., 22.
American Express Co., Inc., 65, Broadway, 6.
Olympic Airways, Room 1210, 655 Madison Avenue, 21.

books . . .

Bonnard, André — *Greek Civilization, from the Iliad to the Parthenon.*
Bury, John B. — *A History of Greece to the Death of Alexander the Great.*
Cottrell, Leonard — *The Bull of Minos.*
Graves, Robert — *The Greek Myths.*
Huxley, Michael — *The Root of Europe, Studies in the Diffusion of Greek Culture.*
Kitto, H. D. F. — *The Greeks.*
Lessing — *Laocoon.*
Nietzsche — *The Origin of The Tragedy.*
Quennell, M. & C. H. B. — *Everyday Things in Ancient Greece.*
Warner, Rex — *The Vengeance of the Gods.*
Webster, T. B. L. — *Art and Literature in fourth-century Athens.*

Modern Greece

Durrell, Lawrence — *Reflections on Marine Venus.*
Finlay, G. — *History of Greece from its Conquest by the Romans to the Present Time, 1877.*
Forster, E. S. — *A Short History of Modern Greece, 1941.*
Golding, Louis — *Goodbye to Ithaca.*
Kazantzakis, Nicos — *Zorba the Greek.*
Christ Recrucified.
Krippner, Monica — *Beyond Athens: Journeys through Greece.*
Leigh-Fermor, Patrick — *Mani.*
Miller, Henry — *The Colossus of Maroussi*
Powell, Dilys — *An Affair of the Heart.*
Warner, Rex — *Eternal Greece, Views of Attica.*

photographs . . .

Georges Viollon, pp. 2, 8, 9, 66, 94, 105, 112, 113, 114, 115, 119, 122, 136, 138, 141, 145, 146, 150, 151, 154, 157, 169, 170, 173, 179. — David Seymour-Magnum, pp. 2, 11, 70, 73, 74, 75, 76, 85, 86, 101, 107, 108, 127, 135, 166, 178, 181. — Cartier-Bresson-Magnum, pp. 44, 58, 60, 84, 90, 101, 130. — Haas-Magnum, pp. 6, 57, 64, 132, 152, 153, 180. — Anderson-Roger Viollet, pp. 4, 6, 32. — Alinari-Roger Viollet, pp. 12, 182. — Bernard-Roger Viollet, pp. 123, 147. — Roger Viollet, pp. 18, 50, 51, 52, 65, 82, 92, 93, 104, 110, 116, 117, 120, 121, 129, 148 h, 165, 174, 175. — Alinari-Giraudon, pp. 14, 15, 61, 111, 143. — Giraudon, pp. 28, 142, 189. — Cahiers du Cinéma, p. 20 b — Greek Tourist Office, pp. 148 b, 149. — Albertine, p. 142. — Marker, p. 20 m. — William Klein, p. 161. — Radio Times Hulton Picture Library, p. 91.

The photograph on the cover (Ellie Lambeti) is taken from Cahiers du Cinéma.

9863

Printed in Holland by N.V. Grafische Industrie Haarlem